The Guardian of the Sword

By JP Wagner

This is a work of fiction. Similarities to real people, places, or events are entirely coincidental.

THE GUARDIAN OF THE SWORD

First edition. April 30, 2022.

Hardcover edition July 2, 2023

ISBN: 978-1-990862-06-9

Also by J P Wagner

Avantir

The Guardian of the Sword

The Crystal Crown

Talisman Series

Stonecaller

Talisman of the Winds

Standalone

The Search for the Unicorns

Railroad Rising: The Black Powder Rebellion

Maid of the Westermoor

The Wanderpeople

Watch for more at revjpwagner.com.

For Lila of the Plains

Editor's Preface

On the face of it this is just another fantasy novel. But for me this is something more. These were my bedtime stories growing up. This is a whole world that has many legends and languages. This is the first version of the story. As I continue to research my father's work I intend to piece together as many of the legends as possible. If nothing else I am publishing these stories so that they will reach their natural conclusion, to be shared with the world.

- Beth Wagner
February 17, 2022
Burnaby, BC

Introduction

In early 1963, I began to write a quasi-adventure story, the kindest comment on which would be that it was my first effort. I was a young Signalman at the time, posted to Kingston, which provided all the setting for the story. I was posted to Calgary in September of the same year, and about the middle of next March, I was at Rivers, Manitoba, undergoing parachute training. I had borrowed a typewriter from a friend, and resolved to type up this first story, which I did, finishing it just a few days before we made our last jump.

However, it was too long to sell immediately, so I decided to do a short story first, and see what I could do. Upon arriving back at Calgary, I began the story of Rorick and the Sword of Arvandal. As it continued, it became obvious that it was no short story, because I was on page thirty, written longhand on a small writing pad, and still far from finished. I decided to write it up into a book.

As I rode with Rorick and Conel of the Hills on the path of freedom, things came up which had little to do with the story itself. Conel the Wild (Conel of the Hills' ancestor), Cael of the Versek, Icar the Farmer, the Old Island, Garthell, Ferdach Fight, Thumill of the Three Rings, all showed themselves Horagon was mentioned, but not by name, and the story of the Dwarves and the Arkh-bazd Whazar and the Great Green Other People were mentioned briefly. The Vakons were mentioned, and Donal the Bane came to Rorick at Orden. The Elder Folk received a bare mention in the form of Lhorannon (Lhorandon) and Troyan, and Brhandon, along with a few songs identified as "Elder Songs". There were one or two mentions of Ammerlyn, Lhedu Andan (The Wandering Wizard), and a foretelling of

Rorick of the Iron Hand, and the battle against the Darkness.

By the time I had written this book out in longhand, I was already, in my mind, going over the story of Darkon and the Kingship of Avantir. It got me first as a sort of story about the time of the falling of an Empire, but Ammerlyn's coming was tied in with something greater, which finally came out. Anthropology interested me, so I worked out the approximate customs of all the mentioned races, and tied in with it came their languages. It seemed, though, too great en undertaking for one young Signalman with a pen and writing pad.

It would be senseless for me to deny that I was inspired by the work of JRR Tolkien. I was, but not for the plot. I read his "Lord of the Rings" twice, while I was still in Calgary, and after the second time, I was beginning to like them (although they were a bit long). Then, shortly after being posted to Shilo, Manitoba, I bought a typewriter, and wrote out the story of the Hygerian War several times, finally coming up with what I thought was a fairly good story.

However, I was still working out the big story, wishing there was any chance at all for a story as long as it promised to be. Then, "The Lord of The Rings" came out in paperback. On an impulse, I bought them, and this time, and I could see how good it really was. It did more, too. I decided that if one book that size could be written, then the Powers Above, so could another.

So Randell Rode out of Coerl, leaving Malik insane on the throne behind. Darkon watched things happen, from the death of Ross and Kithien to the betrayal of Randell and Ardan by Kedrex, servant of Malik. To Darkon fell the privilege of the barony of Avantir, though it was more like burden. The Sword was his, and the responsibility of uniting the Eastern part of Asbaln to stand along. Ammerlyn, though, had come to help him, and with his counsel, the young Vakon forged a kingdom, but a kingdom which stood by the strength of his Sword-arm alone.

Gorths, Keldhs, Harvatai all swept in to take a piece of Avantir. Brangwyn the Keldh was met by a united war-host, and after a great battle became a part of Avantir. Quird of the Harvatai was beaten and slain in battle, but he left a young son, Terrig, who swore revenge when he became old enough. Cleothen Clutha's son of the Gorths led his men in later, and was beaten back twice. However, Avantir stood strong now, for when Grim Harld's Foster, the adopted brother of Darkon, led a force of Vakon and Halvar Seamen after Rulf Thyrson and his men who settled across the Ilcaniar, Darkon held to his pledge, and led his own men to Rulf's aid. He met Grim and killed him, but they had been raised so much together that, for a time, he lost all will to fight.

Avantir stood while Darkon cared little for life, but Artir, the youngest of the Barons, saw the danger, and spoke to Darkon like a traitor, which made him see where his duty lay. They rode to battle, but bad luck and a mist gave Darkon his first defeat. Cleothen took his refuge in the Marshland, where the cavalry of Avantir was at a disadvantage.

The rebellion of Hyrul of Golden Chain was put down, and Hyrul was brought into the King's service, while aid unlooked for came out of the West; Dertha Arothen's son with the Riders of the Blue Banner. The Derrakos, or Darkos, the wild swamp-dwellers, began to raid out of the swamp, and must be put down. At present, 1967, Darkon is fighting Corsairs and Derrakos, and is hoping yet to be able to drive the Gorths from Avantir before the Second Great War comes.

- JP Wagner

1967

Calgary, AB

Chapter One

Legend surrounds it, and of its origin we have only legends. It is said that the Mountain Dwarfs forged it long ago. But its origin is entwined with the mysterious appearance of Arvandal of Avantir himself, of whom it is known only that he passed through the Mountains to King Coerl and, by the Power of the Sword, aided in quelling the rebellious barons.

The name of the Sword is to be spoken only in the direst peril to the land, when it will answer the call but will almost certainly bring the destruction of he who calls it as well. It is called the Sword Which is Not to be Named, or more simply, the Sword.

On his deathbed, Arvandal said, "The Sword is not for any to wield, but must go to its master. There will be a time when a hero shall draw the Sword and use it in a mighty and desperate war."

His family therefore set the Sword aside until this time and were eventually known as Guardians of the Sword.

One hundred and fifty years later, the Hygerians attacked out of the west. King Gunn, attempting to gather his forces, took refuge east of the Mountains. Fighting in their traditional manner, the men of Asbaln were overwhelmed by the Dark men of the West. The King was killed, his army scattered, and the young Prince was taken to hiding in the Icarian Hills.

The Guardian of the Sword

For five years Avantir was left alone, its position on the edge of the Korochinda Swamp making attack difficult. Then, with the rest of Asbaln firmly under their control, the Hygerians began the siege. For three months the ailing Ardan, with his brother Ross and son Rorick, held out.

- Book of the Sword

Kerran Berandis

"They come again, Lords!" It was not a shout, but the young messenger's voice through the half-empty hall where Rorick was taking his evening meal with his uncle Ross and the other captains of the Guardian's Warriors.

"Which wall?" asked Rorick, buckling on his sword. He was some four inches taller than the tallest in the room, blonde hair over blue eyes, long nose, and thrusting chin reminiscent of Arvandal as seen in his portrait in the Guardian's Quarters.

"The west wall, Milord. And the power lorn Icarians aid them with their bows."

"True barbarians, these Hygerians," declared Rorick as he donned his red-crested helmet, "for who else would choose the hour of the evening meal to launch an assault on our walls?"

The others in the room smiled, then they trooped out to the walls. Ross was at his nephew's elbow. "Two days, three, perhaps a week more," he murmured quietly. "The wielder of the Sword had best come soon, lest there be no more reason for him to come."

As they mounted the walls, Avantir's archers were already using their carefully hoarded supply of arrows. Rorick, his judgement sharpened by the months of siege and assault, could see that the coning fight would be a hard one. He walked along the sector of the wall allotted to his command, exchanging a quiet word here or there with the men. They had all fought together now, common danger making comrades of lord and commoner.

He looked out to the mountains standing tall and blue in the west, and his thoughts went to Draxon, who had been given the responsibility for the Guardian's Pass after the King's magicians had blocked the Old Pass forever. At either end, two hundred men could hold the Guardian's Pass. Draxon, with five hundred, had made not even token resistance. After a night meeting with the Hygerian leaders, he had led his men out to be trapped and killed.

Shortly after this, Gunn of Asbaln, though not yet ready, had led his hosts to Dryx field where they died. For all the great deeds of that day, the valour of Asbaln's men had not been enough to give them victory.

"White the hair that wore the crown,

Old the hand that bore the sword;

Sad the day that foreign warriors

Waded north across Dryx ford."

He remembered the heat and the dust and the noise of that day. He remembered when Gunn's ragged standard had fallen and did not rise again. When Ardan looked at the battered remnant of the contingent, he had led to the battle and said, "All is lost. Let us save what we may."

They had received word later on that some loyal servants had taken the young Prince, Conel, to a hiding place in the Icarian Hills, and it was shortly after this that the first of the Icarians spurned their age-old kinship with the men of Asbaln and offered their services to the Hygerians.

Avantir was strong, for at this point the Ilcaniar River reached the edge of the swamp, and the east wall of the city was just above it. This left three sides to attack from, and the Hygerians were relatively unversed in siegecraft. Their usual tactics against walled cities consisted of continuing to storm the walls until the garrison was too worn down to hold them back, and ferocious unchecked slaughter within the walls of any storm that resisted, to bring others to surrender more easily.

At Avantir, the Icarian archers were making a difference. There were not many of them, but there was no need for many. Avantir's garrison had been near a thousand before Dryx, and the plague, which had struck this past Winter, had cut them to around five hundred.

But the time for musing was past now, with the Dark men swarming up ropes and ladders and the Asbalnians attempting to fend them off. Rorick tried to put himself wherever the need was greatest. But too often found himself having to rally his men to drive back the Hygerians where they seemed to have a foothold.

With the usual suddenness, which Rorick had not gotten used to, it was over. The last Hygerians had retreated down the ladders or had died on the walls, and Asbaln's men slumped exhausted at their posts.

As Rorick was completing his assessment of the result, along with Ross, whose grim face told his own thoughts, a messenger found him. "The Guardian wishes to speak with you, Milord."

Dismissing the messenger, Rorick descended the stone stair into the courtyard. Then entered the inner keep where his father lay. The man on the bed only resembled superficially the warrior who, by the force of his will, had brought the remnant of his force back from the red ruin of Dryx field. Brought them back in a running fight with the Hygerians. "How do we stand, my son?"

"We have four hundred and twenty-three presently able to bear arms, perhaps one hundred fifty of them unwounded. We have thirty who will not fight for some weeks, if ever. And we have another hundred or so nearly healed from their wounds, who will be able to fight again shortly.

"With the luck of Thumill of the Three Rings, we might stop two more attacks such as tonight's. May the Dragons of Lycar hunt the Icarians! And if the next attack is pressed with great determination, we will go down. If the Wielder of the Sword is indeed to come to give aid in a mighty and desperate war, then this one is as mighty and as desperate as he could wish."

His father sighed. "As I had thought," he said, "But I needed to have it said for certain. Well, the time has come at last. Help me from this cursed bed."

"Father—-"

"If I die now through rising from this bed, or die tonight hacked to bits by Hygerian blades, what difference will it make? But I tell you, we must try to keep the Sword from their hands if it lies in our power. Now help me!"

In that instant, he was Ardan of Avantir, Guardian of the Sword. His orders were to be obeyed. Rorick helped him up, and they went down into the storeroom in the lower levels of the keep, and into a room beyond that. Within that room was a small wooden table, upon which lay a sword, plain enough in appearance save for the ruby in the pommel, cased in a similarly plain scabbard.

Ardan leaned momentarily against the doorjamb, then pulled himself erect. "Where is your responsibility, Rorick? Take it, wear it, until the hero finds you."

Rorick shook his head in refusal, "Why can't you carry it with you?"

"No, no, we know that I am dying," replied Ardan, "that there is no hope of my taking it away safely. *My* lot shall be to surrender the castle."

"Surrender Avantir?" Rorick touched the hilt, wooden, bound by three brass rings, then began to belt on the Sword. "You will allow the home of our fathers to pass into the hands of the barbarians while there are yet warriors capable of fighting?"

Ardan sighed. "What point is there in killing the last of our Warriors to delay the entry of the Hygerians for a few hours? Better they should live and try to join with Conel in the Hills."

"But the Sword! They know of it, and will never let it leave here even though we surrender."

"Before the surrender, you will take it and most of the remaining warriors away to join with Conel."

With all these shocks following one on another, Rorick was silent for a time. Before he could speak, Ardan continued, looking directly into his eyes. "Yes, that cursed pride of yours forbids your leaving the castle before the last blow is struck. I tell you, Rorick, your task and responsibility is to take the sword end bring it to Conel in the Hills, to be with him until the Wielder comes."

Then, as though the argument were over, he turned to a portion of the wall. "Look over here."

He pushed a loose stone in the wall with his hand, and moved a second with his foot, then pushed on the wall. After a moment's fruitless effort, he stopped. "Put your shoulder to the wall here."

Rorick complied and nearly fell on his face as a section of the wall swung back to reveal dark corridor. “There,” said Ardan, “is the way out of Avantir. It comes out in a small house in the Swamp, from whence you shall have to make your way around the rear of the Hygerian camp. I would suggest that you and your men go in small groups, by widely separated routes, to avoid their scouts. “

“Father, I am under your orders and I obey. But must tell you that I very much dislike this business of skulking off and leaving home to be conquered. I see my duty to Avantir.”

“Duty! Your duty is the Guardianship of the Sword. I know not when or how the Wielder will appear, but it is your task and your duty to care for the Sword until it is required. Now let us go back.”

Having shut the door, they returned to Ardan’s room, where Ross joined them. Ardan explained the plan to him, and he nodded, saying, “It is as well; all we could do now is kill more men for no purpose. I will select the group to go with you, Rorick, the best and steadiest men so far as possible. Sunrise tomorrow?”

“The sooner the better,” said Ardan, “I hope that we have not already waited too long.”

It was dark, Rorick judged about midnight, when one of the Warriors shook him awake. “An attack prepares, Milord. On all sides save the River, and the Icarians are spending arrows like the gold of a drunken sailor. In this light, they can expect to hit with one in twenty.”

“After today’s attack, they come so soon again? They must be confident of success.” Rorick was dressing swiftly. “How do the men take it?”

Young Tumell said, “If they are truly coming from all sides, how do they think to escape us this time?”

Rorick grinned, fastening the last buckles on his harness. He strapped the Sword to his waist and his own blade, then took up his shield and strode out. He went up to the walls, taking the steps two at a time. It was then that he heard the scraping as ladders went up against the walls and the clink as grappling hooks found their hold on the stone.

Then the dark helms showed over the ramparts. The dark faces showed below them, and swords glimmered and shimmered like pools of moonlit water. Now the noise of battle began as sword met sword, and shields rang under hard blows.

The Guardian's Warriors were stretched thin to hold the whole of the wall. Though they fought like the heroes of the Elder Legends, here and there, the dark ones found a foothold.

Three times Rorick rallied small bands of Warriors to destroy such footholds before they could be strengthened. And each time he saw another breakthrough before he was done. And each time, the Warriors available to deal with the situation were fewer.

Then, following his third success, he looked around him as he leaned on his blade, huffing. Was it growing pale in the West already? Powers above, how long had they been at this? In four places that he could see, black cloaks and black helms and spiked shield-bosses ruled the wall. While down in the courtyard, Ross and a handful of others were keeping the Hygerians from the gate.

Then Hygerians were advancing on them with harsh yells and bright blades, and he had to fight for his life. When he had respite again, his available force was small indeed. While in the courtyard, Ross stood fighting alone, forced aside from the gates, while flickering torches painted the scene a bloody hue. The shouting hordes were swarming in the open gates.

Even as Rorick watched, his uncle fell, but around him was a noble corpse's guard of enemies. There was another battle going on as well, on the steps of the inner keep. With a start, Rorick saw it was his father, bearing only sword and shield, but fighting well. But pride, strong will, and remembered skill can only partly make up for a body weakened by illness and fever, and Rorick knew himself to be the last of Arvandal's line.

He remembered too, the take and burden laid on him by his father, that the Sword should be brought to Conel in the Hills. But as he looked around, the swarm of Hygerians made that task seem impossible of achievement. After a moment, he said:

"Arvandal's line were warriors all,

And his House was born in strife;

Should I succeed, or should I fail,

I have lived a warrior's life."

He turned then to the five Warriors left to him. "My friends, my brothers, Avantir is lost. There is one more thing which I must attempt. You owe me no further service; go now, and may the Powers go with you."

One of the Warriors bowed and said, "Guardian, we did not agree to serve you merely when victory was ours. Where you go, there go we also, though death should wait at the road's end."

Rorick returned the bow. "Come, then."

They moved in behind him and struck the first Hygerians like a thunderbolt. The enemy were a small group, and Rorick's band cut through them as much by force of will as by arms. They made for the nearest stairway to the courtyard. When they reached it, however, descent was clearly impossible, for it was crowded with Hygerians coming up. They continued to move along.

Rorick now had only two Warriors left, and when they had fought their way past the next group of enemies, he was alone, with more barbarians advancing toward him. He could not possibly reach the next stairway.

He saw one slim chance remaining to him; gripping his sword firmly, he ran toward them. Then, just out of sword-range, he vaulted up into an embrasure of the wall. From there, Rorick sprang to the merlon and ran along the top of the wall, passing the first of the stupefied Hygerians before they were aware of what was happening.

Suddenly, short Hygerian javelins flew at him. As he leaped between merlons, he was forced to dodge one that threatened to come too close, a movement which caused him to land off-balance. Hopping sidewise to retain his balance, he missed his footing and began to fall towards the waters gleaming darkly below.

Rorick released his sword and shield. Then he contrived to turn his fall into some sort of dive. The weight of the Sword and the war-shirt on his back carrying him all the way to the muck at the bottom of the water. He thanked the Powers that the spring had been a wet one, and the waters deep. He was a strong swimmer and was thus able to bring himself to the surface somewhat beyond the light of the torches which were being cast down from the walls.

"Ah, they want to be sure of me, then. That is a compliment, I think." At last, weary with the exertion, he pulled himself out onto a moderately wet bank. Thinking of finding some kind of shelter before morning, lest the enemy send parties to search for him, he pushed and plundered his way through bush and deadfall until he fell against a mound of earth in the centre of a grove. His questing fingers found what was most certainly a door, covered in cobwebs.

Finding the latch, he opened the door and carefully felt his way inside. There was no light at all, but he ran against something soft, a bundle of cloth which he finally made out to be cloaks. Opening the bundle, Rorick removed his sodden garments. Then he wrapped himself in a cloak and dried his armour as well as he could with another. Then spread another two on the floor to make a bed of sorts. Rorick lay down and, despite his certainty that sleep would be long in coming, was asleep very soon.

Chapter Two

Men had come from all Asbaln and beyond to see if the Sword might be theirs. But the family of the Guardian had been content only to guard it, keeping it while man after man failed to bring the Sword from its sheath. The ambiguity of Arvandal's prophecy had led them to think of themselves only as caretakers until the time that the foretold hero should come. Some have said that the prophecy, by that same ambiguity, led to the fall of Avantir.

-Book of the Sword

Kerran Berandis

In the morning, opening the door to let in light, Rorick was amazed. All around the walls were racks of weapons and armour, most of the blades carefully wrapped in oiled cloth. Obviously, someone had considered the possibility of arming a small war-host. A closer look revealed something else of interest. The styles of decoration and the forms of the helmets showed that the bulk of the material there was of the era of Arvandal. Some of the perishable items, war-cloaks and the like, were newer, and he suspected that Guardians through the years had augmented and replaced certain items there.

He found a good sword which fit his hand, a helmet which felt right on his head, and a shield as well. He took a bow and a quiver full of arrows, and completed his equipment with a five-foot spear, suitable for thrusting or throwing, and set out.

Outside, there was something unexpected. A small rowboat lay beside the mound. The boat was in reasonable condition, though a bit dry, and if Rorick used it, he would be doing a good deal of bailing.

It was certain, though, that using it would be preferable to going overland. He set the boat in the water.

Before stepping into it, Rorick glanced back through the thick trees at the turrets of Avantir. "Well, father, I came here by a route other than the one you had shown me, but I am here."

Here, so near the mouth of the river, the current of the Ilcaniar was weak. As Rorick was rowing against the current, toward the Icarian Hills unseen beyond the gnarled trunks of the swamp-trees, he looked down on the face of the shield on the bottom of the boat, at the emblem of Avantir upon it, the leather gloved fist holding the Upraised Sword.

"Fair towers of Avantir, I go, I go,

Fair towers of Avantir, I grieve.

Home of my heart, great is my sorrow,

For bound by my duty, I leave.

Ye folk of the East land, stand forth, stand forth,

Ye folk of the East land, take heart.

The Red Dragon sleeps where Icar's folk dwell,

And the Sword is awaiting its part."

The journey was not easy. For though Rorick was not forced to follow the twists and turns of little-used paths, he had to fight the current of the River, and had to stop to bail out the boat several times lest it sink completely.

Of the wild Derrakos of the swamp, he saw no certain sign. He thought on several occasions that certain flashes of movement which touched the corner of his eye might have been watchers of that mysterious people, and one night he was kept awake until dawn by a continued eerie chanting among the trees.

In two days, he was out of the Swamp. By now, the planks of the boat had swelled enough that he was no longer forced to bale so frequently. Still, all the area for miles on either side of the main river-channel was marsh. Though the marsh held none of the dread mystery of the Swamp, where old dark trees, hung and looped with moss and vines, resembled prisoners of some sorcerer, turned into chained statues at his whim. The marsh was still tedious to pass through. Only in scattered places were there more than a few yards of relatively dry ground, and rarely was it elevated enough to allow him to see over the miles of tall marsh-reeds. The marsh was a lonely and comfortless place.

During all this journey, constantly turned his mind to the problem of the Hygerians. Surely there must be a way to defeat them. Surely there must be tactics available to the Asbalnians which would give them the victory. Idea after idea he considered, many he rejected, others he reserved for more consideration.

By the middle of the fourth day from departing Avantir, the current was becoming too strong to row against, though by now he was nearly in the Hills. Abandoning the boat, he set out on foot. He had some idea of where the prince might be, though with some of the Icarians having sold out to the Hygerians, nothing was certain.

That night, just as Rorick had finished making his fire, he looked up to see a troll step into the small circle of light. Its appearance was like that of many of its kind. A race of which Rorick had seen only two at a distance. The troll stood half again the height of a man, with green, hairless skin, arms hanging to the knees, a snarl, a stench, and a light of flaming madness in the eyes.

It was not impossible to kill a troll, but it was very difficult. The only wound which would not heal in an instant would be one to the heart. Yet few could come to close quarters to make the necessary thrust, and fewer still could survive.

Then too, none could outrun a troll, so battle was the only chance, no matter how slim. Rising, Rorick threw his spear. The beast grinned, pulled the spear from the wound, and cast it aside. Stepping in, Rorick struck with his sword as the troll moved. The blade carved through its shoulder halfway down the chest. The massive tree-trunk bulk of the other arm strung, catching Rorick's shield to send spinning backward, his sword flying free from his grasp.

Half stunned, he rolled aside as the beast rushed in with a noise which must have been a cry of triumph. Rorick came to his feet; his sword lay over against a rock, the blade broken off some inches above the hilt. A few feet away, beside the fire, the Sword lay in its scabbard. He leaped for the Sword and had his hand on it moments before the troll's latest rush brought it pounding up behind him.

With no thought of what to do with a sheathed sword, save perhaps to use it as a club, he whirled and brought the Sword up to a guard position. The Sword swung free from its sheathe. He felt a light tingling in his hand, and was shocked into momentary immobility while the troll, after an instant's pause, flung itself at him with wide open arms.

The instant in which he was allowed to react gave Rorick only time to step forward in a thrust aimed at the green chest, then dodged aside as the large body crashed forward, almost trapping him. He thought, for a moment, that the beast cried out in a nearly intelligible voice, just before it died.

He was not sure how long he stood there afterwards, staring at the blade glowed gently with its own inner light. Thoughts chased through his mind; might he have saved Avantir, had he known that the Sword was his to wield? Might he not even have saved the day earlier, at Dryx field? Or was it perhaps that the Powers had allowed for this in their grandiose plans?

But wielding the sword would definitely make the raising of a war-host in the Hills a possibility.

"Arvandal rode out armed for war,

The bared blade raised up on his shield;

The knave who stole his lady love,

Was slain because he thought to yield.

Then other foes fenced in the maid,

And sterner men set bar and ward,

But cleaned the blade mud smote and flashed,

And towers reeled before the Sword."

Chapter Three

Then said Wise Icar, "We must go from these plains to the hills in the north. There shall we be able to hold a lend safe from the Bowmen in the Iron Coats, and be far from the war which they pursue against the Little Ones and the Other People."

Then the people gathered, and they numbered near five hundred, men and women, and many children as well, of the Hunter people as well as the farmers whose forefathers had fled the Old Island on the Night of Fire.

All these had united in an attempt to survive the war which was raging in the land. Far into the hills they marched, and established there the first of their villages.

On the night of the second clay from their arrival, they beheld in the sky the flare of the dread magic called the Little Sun, as it was released on the far side of the Mountains. Icar alone knew it for what it was.

"Here we stay," he declared, "and hold these hills in peace, if it may be so, or by war if we must, but war shall not be of our seeking."

-The Hill People's history Randell Eagle-claw

Noon of the second day from the battle with the troll found Rorick crouched in the shelter of a bush at the crest of a hill overlooking a village of considerable size. From his limited and second-hand knowledge of the Hills, he guessed this ought to be Carill Don, the Chief Village of the Icarians, reputed to have remained faithful to their traditional friendship with the folk of the Plains.

He had been watching for some time, and had yet to see any persons in the village who looked to be other than Icarians. It might be, however, that Asbalnians in the Hills who preferred to remain inconspicuous might take on native dress. Carill Don was the most likely place for the Prince to be, though who could say for sure? With Icarians selling themselves to the barbarians.

It might even be that the fall of Avantir, Asbaln's last fortress, would have brought the Icarians to acceptance of Hygerian sovereignty, and walking into this village might be walking into the hands of his enemies.

Grinning slightly, he said:

"Delay but weakens warrior hands,

Binds the heart in iron bands;

Are they friends or are they foe?

Wishing will not make it so."

Standing, he tucked his hands into his belt and walked down toward the village. There were sudden noises of mild alarm, and he was met by a group of armed men.

They showed no hostility, only watchful caution, and he said, "I seek Prince Conel of Asbaln. Can anyone here direct me to him?"

There were mutterings among them, in their own language, which was that of the Derrakos of the Swamp, though with several Asbalnian words, usually pronounced in a fashion to render them nigh unrecognizable. One moved off, and went quickly among the huts; several others put arrows to bows and went back up the slope towards where Rorick had been hidden; the rest stayed watching him and waiting, occasionally to be joined by others.

Their clothing was mostly skins, though with some wool and linen traded from the lowlands. The men wore kilts and, occasionally, jackets, the women wore knee-length dresses. Their hair was worn Long, in braids, often decked with coloured feathers. The men bore a motley of weapons, spears, swords, and axes, though all carried bows and arrows.

Then a middle-aged man with greying hair pushed through the surrounding circle. "I am Orn, Chief of this village. What we can do for you?"

"I am Rorick of Avantir, guardian of the Sword, and I seek Prince Conel of Asbaln."

"There is word Avantir is fallen."

"Avantir is fallen, but I have brought the Sword hither to Conel. And have important news as well."

"Would you indeed know the Prince if you saw him?"

"Unless the years since Dryx have altered him more than I think likely. And he will know me too. I think he will wish to hear the news I have for him."

"And what news is that, besides that the last of Asbaln's fortresses is fallen, and that his land lies helpless at the mercy of the Hygerians?"

"With respect, Chief, the news must be told to Prince Conel first. You will forgive my caution, but the King does have enemies."

"The 'King,' as you call him, a trifle prematurely, has no enemies in this village. But he will tell you this himself."

A young man, tall and blonde as Rorick, but more slender, stepped through the press. On his jacket was the Red Dragon of the Kings of Asbaln, but needed no such device to aid his recognition. "Milord Prince! Is it well with you?"

"As well as might be, hiding here while enemies roam my land unhindered. And the news that Avantir was fallen appears to mean that they shall continue to do so. While Avantir stood, there was hope; now there is none." Suddenly his expression on changed. "I apologize, Guardian. The loss of Avantir will have meant no less to you than to me."

"If an apology was needed, then I accept. But I think that all is not yet lost."

"No, I see you have brought the Sword away. Yes, I remember being a very small boy when my father asked it be brought to the City of Coerl to allow Gunval Eagle-Sword to attempt to draw it. And I had seen Gunval in action; he was a man to be reckoned with, a warrior of prowess, though he was never one to bully, as happens too often with men who know the ways of weapons better than their fellows. And yet, he could not take the blade from its scabbard for all his strength." He mused on that. "Did you know Gunval is said to have died trying to bring my father's body away from the battlefield?"

"Milord, I bring you more than the Sword. You recognize it, so you can bear witness to this." Rorick drew it from its scabbard and heard the gasp from the assembled Icarians as it glowed in his hand.

Conel smiled at the sight. "Ah, then the hero has come at last. This news shall be worth at least an additional hundred men."

"How many men have you here, Milord?"

"Fewer and fewer. Five hundred came away from Dryx field. Two hundred of those left when Barons Ocar and Nedron went to see if they could raise a rebellion across the Mountains. We heard later when five of them came back that the two barons had died on the way when they met more Hygerians than they had expected. Then as time went on, and less of the land remained free, we lost more men. A few others came in, and we have around two hundred now, though we lost some when they offered peace to all the old barons who would come forward. Lucar and Indabar convinced Briga to go with them, leaving me with a few freeholders to serve as commanders. I must admit to having felt a small degree of pleasure when we learned that it had been a trap to rid the Hygerians of all the Asbalnian nobility. So far as I am aware, you are the last of the barons yet living.

"But you were asking about our strength. As I said, the fall of Avantir took the heart out of many; I have here two hundred men ready to fight, but that is too few."

"It is enough to start with. And if we are able to recruit a few Icarians, I believe we can bring to us a larger force."

"Aye? Then you know the secret magic of the Elder Heroes, that you will summon to your banner the trees of the forest as did Chael, son of Terich?"

"Not quite so easily as that, Milord; we shall have to depend on the might of mortal Men. Will any of the Icarians join us?"

"Aye, many of them, for some suspect the Hygerians will come into the Hills, now that the lowlands are conquered, and others seek to wipe out the shame they feel for those of their countrymen who forsook the ancient bond between our races. In the time it would take for me to raise my voice and ask, we could have fifty, and within seven weeks we could have five hundred."

"It is well. Think on this, then. We cannot defeat a large force of Hygerians with much less than equal numbers. However, if we send out fast parties to raid, to destroy scouts and foraging parties, we can cut them down little by little without their being able to bring the weight of their numbers to bear.

"And, if we are able to field a small force of bowmen, all mounted, we will have a snail group able to hit and run before a garrison can organize to fight back. We can challenge their control of the lowlands nearby, and recruit more men on the strength of that, until we are able to meet them in open battle."

"And where will these horses come from?"

"We will get what we can from our lowland herdsmen at the first and take them from the Hygerians later."

"Ah, so you have thought of everything, then?"

"I have tried, Milord Prince."

A swift smile lighted the prince's features. "Formalities are for others. To you, I am Conel, and shall call you Rorick, and let the enemies of Asbaln beware. Would that my father had had counsellors of your sort. When had you planned to take the first horses?"

"Tonight, if it is possible.

"Aye, I think we might raise a small party for tonight. And I think it would be best if we do it secretly. For the longer it is before the Dark Ones suspect our plans, the better it will be."

They found twenty Icarians who could ride horses, and that evening they went down into the lowlands. They acquired twenty horses, and remained in hiding until the next evening, camped in a grove of trees, eating cold rations. A patrol of twenty Hygerians rode by, and Rorick and his party watched in silence. When the dark-clad men were out of sight, Rorick turned to Conel. "We will not hide thus for long. Indeed, we will not be able to. You remember what that farmer said, the one from whom we got the last four horses? 'I will do for you what I may, but if it should be that the Hygerians show themselves to be masters of the land, then I shall have to submit to their rule. I am not a man to let myself be killed for an ideal which is not attainable.'"

Conel nodded. "Too true. 'In victory your friends are an army, in defeat only the dead support you.' We may gather horses in this manner for a week, perhaps two, then they shall begin asking if we intend to actually fight, or only lurk in the Hills."

From almost the moment they returned to Carill Don, the Icarians were practicing at horseback archery. As a beginning, they learned to shoot from a standing horse, eventually working from a walking mount. Even for expert bowmen, it was not a simple feat. Perseverance brought eventual skill.

About midmorning, a hunter came running in to report a small band of armed and armoured Asbalnians making their way toward the town. The report said that the men bore the upraised Sword on their shields, a fact which brought the Guardian of the Sword out expectantly.

There were ten of them, and their leader was a short, somewhat stout, grizzled man, whose quick movements belied the thickness of his girth. As they approached, the expressions on their faces went from disbelief to amazement to joy, then they stopped, drew well-used swords from their scabbards, raised them, and clashed them across their shields. Then they were crowded around Rorick and all talking at once, asking the same question in varying form.

It was their leader finally brought them to order, and Rorick then answered the question. "Yes, I fell from Avantir's wall at the end of the fight, but fell into the water. I made my way through the Swamp to the Hills, and discovered on the way that it is for me to bear the Sword. Now, Beran, son of Ralf, tell me your tale."

"When you fell from the wall, I led a band who were willing to try to fight their way out. Twenty-three of us attacked the gate, seventeen of us passed it, and we ten were able to reach the forest. Of course, the barbarians were more concerned to take the castle than to chase down small bands of fugitives, so they did not pursue far. We decided we would seek the Prince in the Hills to give him what aid we could. To the Powers, be thanks for your safety, Milord Guardian."

"And for yours, Beran the Swift. Now come; we have the beginnings of an army here, and will need your experience."

The two hundred lowlanders in the Hills at the time were the dedicated core of the greater number who had been there until despair and disillusionment drove them forth. The coming of the Sword was sufficient to prevent any further desertions, and indeed, a trickle of young men arrived seeking their Lord, Prince Conel.

And Rorick explained his new ideas to the men who would train the army, eventually convincing most of them of the efficacy of his methods.

Chapter Four

Saddle your horse and string your bow;
Horsemen forth! To the plains we go!
A cup for the journey, a cup at its end,
A cup to remember a fallen friend,
A cup to the King and Avantir's Lord,
And a cheer for the bearer of the Sword.
—Cavalry song, attributed to Helana of the Hills

Rorick soon had the Icarians practicing mounted archery so assiduously that some complained. He was unmoved. The Hygerians would not rest long while the heir to Asbaln's throne was at large, and the host which had been occupied at Avantir was now freed.

Then too, there was the matter of the Honour of the Hills. Three brave fellows were sent out to live in the Marshland and prey on the Hygerians, spreading a rumour that the King had moved from the Hills because it was too well—known that he was there, and it was expected that the Hygerians would now move into the Highlands, now that the Lowlands were conquered.

It served the purpose, keeping the Hygerians from concentrating their forces immediately. A week from the time of their first expedition, Rorick took ten of the most adept of the Hillmen and went down to gather horses on the plain.

Again, they went by night, and again they camped in concealment by day, and they stayed out for two nights. On the third night, with a herd of seventy-nine under their less than expert control, they set out back to the Hills. Suddenly, their scout was riding back to them to warn them that a party of Hygerians was approaching. It was a patrol comprising ten mounted men, riding directly on the trail toward them.

It would be impossible to move off the trail with the whole herd, so they would have to fight. Leaving two men to guard the horses as yell as possible, Rorick took the rest down the trail in two columns. Suddenly, just as the Hygerians were becoming aware that the approaching party was not of their people, Rorick led one column out to the right, Conel led his column to the left, and they galloped down, loosing arrows at little more than sword range.

Six Hygerians fell. The others, not realizing how heavy their losses had been, took their long fourteen—foot lances and turned to ride after the Horsemen, who had rallied a little down the trail. Loosing more arrows, they swerved right and left away from the then rode to pursue the last of the Hygerians as they fled.

In the pursuit, one slightly wounded Hygerian who had his horse killed, took a javelin from the case at his saddle and threw it, with more haste than aim. It gashed Rorick's left arm, but not seriously enough for him to pay attention to until the last of the enemy was dead.

They rounded up seven of the Hygerian horses, and by some great fortune, the guards had only lost two of the seventy-nine in their care, so that they were understandably jubilant when they entered the village with the paleness of dawn. People crowded around to hear how their exploits had gone, and to admire the war-gear taken from the Hygerians, and to take the horses to be corralled.

Helana, daughter of Orn, was among the crowd. Rorick had noticed her occasionally, had even met her briefly one day, but his continual dashing from one group of men to another, demonstrating, explaining, and convincing, had left him with little more than her name. She approached him, noting the comer of the cloak wrapped around his forearm.

"Will you allow me to see to that?"

"It is nothing, lady, only a scratch."

"Indeed. And I have seen wound—poisoning arise from scratches of that sort before. I think we can ill afford to lose you. Cone."

After a moment's hesitation, Rorick followed her into one of the nearby huts where she busied herself with herbs, warm water, and cloths. "You are Helana, daughter of Chief Orn, are you not?"

"I am. We met once, but you had to leave suddenly to make clear to someone how a small force of infantry could defeat twice their number. I am surprised that you remember me."

"You are one to be remembered. You speak as though this war were your own."

"If it is not yet, it will be. I think that only a few fools believe that the Hygerians will be satisfied with Asbaln and leave us to our Hills. I, for one, distrust Razak, and fear him. In the long-gone years, Great Icar led our people into these Hills out of war and slaughter on the plains below. Since then, we have held these Hills; Ilach the Rash, son of Conel the Wild, sought to take us for a part of his kingdom, and discovered that we had more arrows than he had warriors. Besides that, barbarians from the Wild Lands seeking to reach Asbaln often faced us. So we are not unused to war here, and when Razak comes, he will find us ready.

"But would you not yourself advise us to fight while we may count on some aid from Asbaln? Therefore, the war is ours as much as yours, though there are nearsighted fools who would see it otherwise." She smiled suddenly. "You will pardon my vehemence, but I have heard my father say this same thing to many people. Now, tell me of your journey to the plains."

"What of it? We rode mostly at night, and hid during the day, and we fought only the once, when there was no choice."

Despite the disclaimer, they found things to talk of for some time.

Word of the skirmish got round, and soon there were numbers of young men coming round to offer their bows to the service of the King and the Guardian. On the next day, hunters brought in a party of young men from the lowlands, thirty of them, come to offer their swords to the Prince.

For some time, establishing his system of training kept Rorick occupied. He knew well what he wanted, and the Prince understood rapidly enough, as did some of his officers, but many did not, and it was necessary to be continually going from party to party, explaining and re-explaining the methods he wished them to use, the reasons for doing so, and in the last extremity, simply bullying them.

Within two weeks, they had found a group of men who not only comprehended the new methods, but the reasons behind them. From these, they recruited some commanders, putting them in charge of training, to make clear the reasons for the new methods, or if necessary, to instill their methods by command.

Still, they continued to send parties down to the plain for horses, avoiding aggressive action when possible. However, the Hygerians set up a post outside the town of Virdan. They built a log stockade and established a small garrison. It seemed clear enough that they were making a beginning at sending an expedition into the Hills.

Chapter Five

For every new thing which Rorick and Conel introduced in the training of their war-host, there are those who will point to a place in history when that same method was used before. The differences usually are that Rorick and Conel applied these techniques on a large scale, or that they caused them to succeed.

But because of the necessity of developing a cavalry force, it was soon impossible to keep the Hygerians unaware of the host gathering in the Hills. It was therefore necessary to make a careful judgement between attacking before they were well—enough trained and hesitating until the Hygerians were prepared.

The Hygerian War
Randell of Avantir.

One day, Rorick and Conel led eighty men out against the garrison of Virdan, with private misgivings carefully hidden. It was two weeks since the first reports of the building activity at Virdan, and while they might have wished to have their Horsemen somewhat more practiced, they could not allow the Hygerians to establish fortified camp below the Hills. Partly because it made possible patrolling which would prevent access to the Hills from much of the Lowlands, partly because of the lowering of morale which it would bring. They must attack.

When they arrived at the hill overlooking the fortress, they found they were a trifle late. Except for one small gap, which was blocked by wagons, the palisade was up. They paused only for a short time to make some final adjustments to their plan of attack. It was rather a dark night, but their plans had been predicated on close—range fighting.

As they looked down on their objective, Conel turned to Rorick,

"Who will ride with me this night?

Who is with me in this fight?

Bitter and deep lie Asbaln's woes,

Who will ride against her foes?"

Rorick replied:

"Bitter indeed are Asbaln's woes,

Fierce and numerous are her foes;

Behold, My Lord, with thee we ride;

Close as shield upon thy side."

The two smiled at each other, then the Prince gave his signal. A small group rode down opposite to the gap in the palisade, carrying small, closed jars suspended by long cords. When they were fairly close, they reined in their horses. Taking the cords, they swung the jars around their heads and let them fly into the fort, directed generally at the buildings and piles of stores within.

It was only then that the guards, perhaps believing them to have been a late-arriving group of Hygerian reinforcements, sounded the alarm. The jars struck and broke against buildings and other hard surfaces, releasing hot coals closely packed with dry grass, which immediately burst into flames. At the same time, other Horsemen were kindling balls of pitch on the heads of certain arrows, and loosing them into the fort as well.

As the alarm vent up, still others of the Horsemen shot with care and precision at any who showed themselves. The Hygerians, not a folk particularly used to cities, fortresses, or such enclosures, had had almost no preparations for fire, and soon confusion was rampant. Some sought to defend the fort against the attackers, some sought to put out the fires, and some tried to do both.

A group of Horsemen rode in with ropes and cast loops onto the wagons, blocking the gap. With others of their number using bows to keep the Hygerian heads down, they pulled several of the vehicles out of place. The Hygerians were rushing to prevent their coming in the gaps, but the dread Icarian arrows struck any who dared appear in the open.

Now, with confusion still reigning, the Horsemen entered the fort and began a rampage. The Hygerians were totally unable to organize to meet this new threat, and soon had ceased to attempt to hold the fort. In little groups, by twos or threes singly, they made their attempts to escape to the brush outside. Not a great number succeeded.

The Horsemen packed as much of the arms and equipment as they could salvage before the fires became too hot and dangerous, and left the rest to burn. Rorick, grabbing a place on his cheek where a hot ember had landed, looked at Conel. “Well, we have done it.”

“We have indeed. If they had had more archers, it would have been much more difficult. We lost six men, five of them to javelins. By the time we got to close quarters, the battle was ended. But how often will we be able to fight our enemies at night, silhouetted against fires?”

“Probably never again. But we will find other methods.”

“We must. Well, let us be off; the town of Virdan will supply proper bandages and medicines for our wounded, and think a little food would be in order.”

In the Market Square of Virdan, on the Proclamation Board, they placed a large notice to inform the people that the King was in the Hills with his host, and that the Wielder of the Sword had come. It also bid every willing man come to join them in the struggle, and was signed not only with Conel’s name, but with the Red Dragon of Asbaln.

The local innkeeper was unwilling to open his door at the first, but when the choice was put to him of opening it or having it smashed down, he was more agreeable. They ate much of his stored food, and his supply of ale suffered as well, but they paid for it in Hygerian golden jewellery.

They sent him out first of all, to find appropriate material for bandaging wounds, leaving his somewhat flustered wife to see to the other sorts of provisions. Though some of the younger members of the company jested gently at the innkeeper and his wife, and the small crowd of villagers who gathered in curiosity, the general tone was one of friendliness. Indeed, many of the Horsemen were known personally to the people of Virdan, for Virdan was one of the towns in which Icarian hunters traded for Lowland goods.

And the fact that they paid for what they took convinced the people that this was no mere band of bandits, while a couple of old veterans who had made their way from the red ruin of Dryx Fight swore that they recognized the Prince. Finally, drawing the attention of the people to where smoke still rose from the ruins of the Hygerian fortress in the paleness of the new dawn, Rorick drew the Sword from its scabbard.

There was no doubt in anyone's mind as to what they saw, for the blade glowed with a light of its own, and their respect for the Sword told them that only such a weapon could have this property. They gave a cheer for the King, a cheer for the Guardian, and another for his Icarian allies. The Horsemen mounted and rode away in a long double column. As their hoofbeats died away in the distance and as they began to disappear over the rise, the people turned to each other, as though for assurance that they had actually seen what they had seen.

A week later, Rorick and a band of twenty Horsemen were out on a long patrol intending to pick up what horses they could, and fighting any Hygerian patrols they came across. Suddenly, they found themselves facing a force of about a hundred Hygerian infantry. They were about half spearmen and half archers, and they marched along the trail below the hill from which he looked down on them.

Clearly, to charge on them would be to give them time to take up a formation with spearmen in front and archers shooting over their heads. Such a formation would allow them to dispose of Rorick's much smaller force practically at leisure. Yet, he hated to have to allow them to pass unmolested, to have to ride to the Hills for help. A plan came to him; he gave some quick instructions to his men and waited as about half of them set off to take a position behind the barbarians.

Then he led the remainder of them over the crest of the hill, coming at the double column of infantry on a dead run. The enemy reacted with speed, spearmen moving to form a double line of bristling spearpoints while the archers took up a similar formation behind them, waiting for the proper range.

At extreme range, Rorick and his group halted. They launched a few arrows, but shooting downhill at that range was difficult, and none hit home. Then, as the Hygerians hesitated about what to do next, the rest of the Horsemen came galloping around the hill. They swept down the line, shooting into the Hygerians from ranges of six to ten feet.

The enemy tried to turn and answer them, but some were concerned with Rorick's group, which was moving again. Confusion was in command; some turned, some did not, and after firing more arrows into them, both groups charged home. The Hygerians broke up and fled. About fifteen spearmen and a similar number of archers formed into a circle and made their way toward a small grove of trees, moving steadily and determinedly, the archers loosing arrows at any Horsemen who approached, while the spearmen prevented any consideration of charging home. The Horsemen concentrated on those of less steady temperament.

About escaped, near ten more into the grove of trees, making it nearly impossible for the Horsemen to attack them successfully. Rorick and his group contented themselves with gathering as much of the Hygerian equipment as they could carry, particularly the armour. They had lost four men in the battle, but the gain in equipment and morale made it a good trade.

Within the next three weeks, they were out raiding against outposts and garrisons, attacking any patrols they came across. A few garrisons were wiped out, some others were so weakened as to find it necessary to withdraw.

As they extended their activities, it became more difficult to keep their entire force mounted. They had taken all the horses they could from the nearest lowland areas, while the Hygerians had been even more forceful in replacing their losses from the local farms. The situation was such that any party of Horsemen would attack almost any party of Hygerian cavalry hoping to acquire one or two horses.

In the meantime, men from the lowlands were making their way into the Hills, to seek out Prince Conel and offer their services.

At Carill Don, the Army of Asbaln came into being and grew.

Chapter Six

The Hygerians were always left a little behind in the field of strategy and tactics. It was only after each new method of countering existing Asbalnian attacks was countered in turn and proved disastrous that they were able to begin revising their procedure.

But they did learn, and in the later stages of the war, learned with commendable swiftness. Indeed, had the war lasted even another month, they might have reversed the tide, for they had always the advantage of numbers.

It was for this reason Rorick urged a campaign of speed, trying always to keep the momentum of the attack, always to attack just before the Hygerians were ready.

-The Hygerian War
Randell of Avantir

Not too much later, far-ranging scouts brought in word of a force of six hundred Hygerians marching toward the Hills. They foraged as they came, and the villagers could gain a fairly clear idea of their intentions through casual conversations, which the villagers dutifully passed on to the scouts.

These circumstances presented somewhat of a problem for Rorick and Conel. Neither felt it would be safe to use the infantry yet, but they could not meet so many Hygerians in pitched battle. The Hygerians had not included any cavalry in this force, however. A fact which allowed the Horsemen some advantage.

They divided their force into three groups, Conel having fifty, Rorick fifty, and a young Hillman, Randell, cousin to Helana, led the remaining fifty. They rode out to wear down the Hygerians with continual raids, small ambushes which would cost the enemy a few here and a few there, but never allow them to fight a pitched battle until they were worn down and demoralized.

Somewhere around four hundred Hygerians actually reached the Hills, and by this time only ninety of the Horsemen could ride to meet them. They had more men trained and ready, but they lacked mounts. A great deal of debate went on about the possibility of using their infantry in this battle.

They had somewhat over five hundred, most of them trained to some degree, but there was still concern about their readiness. There was concern, too, about the risk of exposing the fact they had more than a very effective band of mounted raiders before they were completely ready. It was over this point that Conel, Rorick, and Beran met one night in Carill Don. Conel spoke first.

"It is in my mind that we should throw in the infantry and utterly destroy these Hygerians. The infantry would turn the advantage of numbers to our side."

Rorick nodded gravely. "It would do that, but I believe it is too soon. Beran, what do you say of our troops? Could we fight off twice our number of enemies?"

After a moment's frowning consideration, Beran spoke, "I wish, Milord King, that I could say yes to that. But I must be truthful. If one lone Hygerian escapes to report a large force of infantry in the hills, we shall have a thousand Hygerians in the Hills, and several thousand more forming garrisons in the lowlands just below. With the aid of the Icarians, we may keep them from the Hills, but we could never come down, and they need only keep us from the lowlands to prevent our Horsemen from being effective, if only through lack of horses. In another week, I would lead the infantry against up to half again their number.

"So," said Conel softly. "I had feared so. Are they doing well?"

"Aye, Milord King, very well for what they are. You see, we have all young men here, full of fire and fight, who have been ready to give battle since the night they first came here. If we do not let them fight within about two weeks, they will begin to desert and lose their fire. The same will happen if we lose our first battle, or indeed, if we win the first three.

"We require older men, steady men, who can hold the youngsters in line and give them an example to follow."

"Do we have no older men, then?" asked Conel in a mystified tone.

"Aye, Milord King, it is the temper of the Asbalnian farmer. Remember that the Innkeeper at Virdan did not truly believe you were who you claimed to be until he saw the Sword. The word may be out from here to the Southern Sea that Conel is in the Hills with a host, but your farmer will say, "that may be will be, but I'll not leave my farm for traipsing and fighting across the land unless I know surely who I fight for, and that means I must see the King face to face, with his army and all."

He smiled briefly, then continued. "We must take Virdan, or do something equivalent, within two weeks. If we can thus prove ourselves, the older men will come. If not, we will be forced to think again. I will not say that a failure here would doom us. But it would put us under the necessity of reversing the feeling which will grow up about us, that we are not capable of doing that we have set out to do.

"Perhaps in that time we ought to think of hiring a few of the barbarians of the Wild Lands to fight for us."

Conel's eyes flared. "That will I never do! Then I bring wolves over the threshold to drive out the wolves already here, may I be slain like a mad dog! Should we perhaps trade the Hygerians for the Harvatai in their war-carts, with long swords and javelins, ruling our villages with cruelty and terror?"

Rorick smiled slightly. "We will not call the wolves over the border, Conel. We must fight the Hygerians in ways and times and places where they will not expect us. And we must look to finding if there are any in the lowlands who know aught of the construction and garrison of the new fortress of Virdan."

One morning, the whole of the mounted force rode out of Carill Don. About five miles from the village, in an area spotted by clumps of brush, they prepared to meet the enemy. They sent ten men out to remove any scouts who might come near the ambush and warn the main body. Rorick looked at Conel and said,

"A sword, a bow, and a strong swift steed,

And what more does a warrior need?

A comrade riding at his side;

For bare is the back that does brotherless ride."

The Prince grinned and answered,

"A good war-horse beneath the knees;

A banner that blows above in the breeze.

Aye, others have ridden alone, and died;

For bare is the back that does brotherless ride."

Then they clasped hands for an instant, looking into each other's eyes, before Conel turned his horse and rode to his place across the field. Rorick watched him go, the true son of Conel the Wild, whose pride and spirit burned in his eyes.

Far away, Rorick could hear the faint sounds of the skirmishing between his few scouts and the Hygerians. He looked down his line; the state of some of the horses made him shiver with anxiety, but they felt the need to mount as many as they possibly could. He could just see one of the three they had bought from the shifty-eyed Harvatai trader with the horrible accent and the limp.

And as for armour, that was mostly Hygerian manufacture. They had broken off and ground down the spikes from the helmets and shields; it was most important with the helmets, as it was too easy in the dust and confusion of a battle to mistake friend for foe, without the friend wearing something so distinctively of the foe.

Suddenly there was a hot of horses on the far ridge. For a few instants, they milled there, and he could make out the movements as they loosed arrows at the yet unseen enemy.

He sensed the movement that ran down the line and saw that the man next to him had nocked an arrow. He cast another eye over the motley equipment and clothing, the occasional braids peeping out from under helmets, braided with brightly dyed feathers, the fur kilts, even numerous bare feet. What a tatterdemalion army to be challenging the Hygerian might.

And at that moment, the first of the barbarians showed over the ridge, pursuing the fleeing Horsemen. The Horsemen did not flee quick; it being their task to fix the attention of the enemy, preventing them from looking for the hidden ambushers until it was too late. Now the Hygerians blackened the skyline, poured down the slope. The skirmishing Horsemen pulled back farther and farther, still turning to loose arrows into the mass.

Now suddenly the Horsemen were galloping for the brush, and he could see individual Hygerians, dark complexioned faces in an array of expressions, mostly of fierce concentration. The few bowmen among them drew arrows and loosed them in quick, precise movements, advancing a few paces at a time, with the rest of the host advancing behind in what had been a column but was now a crowd. They were sure of battle now, and were anticipating the necessity of coming line.

A trumpet sounded, far across the field where Conel had stationed himself, and Icarian bows lifted, bent, and launched their shafts. Again, there was the shiver of motion along the line as they stooped forward to draw another arrow from their saddle-quivers. Hygerians fell, and arrows continued to fly.

Even so, the Hygerians formed their battle-line. Rorick, drawing his bow and loosing again, muttered to himself, “Now, Randell.”

And then Randell came, galloping down at the Hygerian flank as they moved out into position, twenty men behind him loosing arrows with all the skill they possessed. For this part of the battle, Randell had been assigned the men most proficient at shooting from horseback. They showed it, too, and the Hygerians began an effort to face them.

Randell's group stopped suddenly, wheeled, and rode back, but turned again at the hilltop to shoot down on the Dark ones. Rorick shouted, "Conel and Asbaln!" and urged his horse forward. About half the line was with him, guiding their horses with their knees, holding nocked arrows at full draw until they were very close, then loosing into the Hygerians, who were frantically looking to see if they were actually being flanked on the far side.

As they loosed their arrows, Rorick's force dropped their bows onto the pommels of their saddles, and swords rasped out of scabbards. They clove into the confused Hygerians, many of whom fled already. From this point, Rorick lost sight of what happened elsewhere, for there was a time of desperate hand-to-hand fighting.

The Sword swung and flashed in his hand, and part of his mind heard the ancient cry from the lips of the Icarians, "*Kr Yrriech!* The earth endures!"

Though he could not see what was happening, he knew well enough what ought to be happening. While the Hygerians before him sought to hold firm in the face of the cavalry attack, Conel would continue to shoot into the other flank. At the same time, Randell could lead his own little force down behind the Hygerian line, forcing them to look to their rear as well as their front. Then, when Conel judged them to be sufficiently disordered, he would lead his own force in to the attack.

Dust rose among around the striving, struggling men; iron rang on iron, war-cries rose in the air. It seemed to Rorick that he had led his charge an hour ago, and where were Conel and Randell? Suddenly he was out in the open, and the only Hygerians before him were those fleeing toward the brash.

They pursued them, attacking whenever little groups of them formed to fight, urged by pride or desperation or both, until at last Rorick looked around to find five men following him. He stopped and called them to him. "We are all too scattered. Go, find whoever you can of our men, tell them to rally. The battle is won, and all we can do now is lose badly needed men end horses in fighting foes made strong by desperation."

The battle brought them a good deal of equipment, much of which went to supply their own war-host. Much else went to the limping, shifty-eyed Harvatai trader and some of his colleagues, for the horse situation was now near to critical. They continued their horse-hunting expeditions into the lowlands, though it was more and more difficult to get horses from the farmers.

Chapter Seven

Look to your arms, ye men of the West;
Put your hand to the sword and the bow and the shield;
Come to your rightful King and Lord,
Come from the wood and the herd and the field.
Men of the Mountains, Men of the Sea,
Your land needs your service, your Ring calls you forth;
Many indeed are the foes that face you;
Take shield, take sword, and face to the North!
-Anonymous poem of Asbaln

They set about other activities as well, trying to find out how the fort at Virdan was built, and what its garrison was, and in farther areas seeking to discover what strength the Hygerians could muster against them. An interesting fact emerged; King Razak could not seem to convince his nobles of the danger from the Hills. They would send a few men to him under a commander, but would not come themselves, considering the war to be over.

Small bands of Asbalnians took it upon themselves to harass the Hygerians, some out of loyalty to the King, others simply for the loot they might get from it. The Hygerians, when they could find the perpetrators of such deeds, dealt harshly with them. Sometimes when they could not find the perpetrators, they would deal harshly with the nearest village or farm, as a warning. In any case, it prevented them from putting their full force against Conel and Rorick, lest the entire land rise up behind them when their heavy hand was removed.

But in a short time, five hundred more infantry were marching toward the Hills, supported by three hundred cavalry. The battle to come would not be an easy one. Skirmishes between patrols from the Hills and patrols from Virdan became more and more frequent. Every horse that could possibly be acquired was gained, and colleagues of the Harvatai horse-trader came prepared to sell. Whenever their prices could be met, they were, for the Harvatai horses were usually excellent beasts.

One day, a messenger riding for Virdan was intercepted, and his message brought in. It was written in the Hygerian runes, and the fact that it was written suggested its importance, for this meant that it was not being trusted to the memory of the bearer. The chief magician in the Asbalnian camp, an old man known only as the Old One, was known to have some small skill in the matter of languages, so it was brought to him.

He opened the parchment and looked at it, then at the group of men before him. “It is written in Hygerian runes, but not in the Hygerian language.”

“What does that mean?” asked Randell.

“I know the Hygerian language. I know their writing. The symbols are Hygerian, the language is not...wait!” A smile broke over his features. “It *is* the Hygerian language, but with the letters changed about: Allow me to take some time with it and I shall tell you what it says.”

“Do so, and you shall have our gratitude. It is most clearly something intended to harm us, and if we can be forewarned, so much the better.” Rorick bowed, and they left the magician to his work.

THE PRESENCE OF CALVARY with the Hygerian force advancing on them limited the effectiveness of their typical harassing tactics. Though the Hygerians did not have any mounted bowmen, their cavalry were mobile enough to keep the Horsemen at sufficient distance that the infantry did not suffer heavily. They managed some raids on the enemy while they were camped, very swift attacks which generally served mostly to prove that they were still willing and able to fight.

But arrows were cheaper than men, and from ravines, bushes, rocks and trees, Icarian arrows flew. The watchful Hygerian cavalry, riding to avenge such ambushes, usually found only the places once occupied by the bowmen, and occasionally heard the mocking laughter of the retreating Horsemen.

On the night before they marched forth to battle, Rorick addressed the infantry.

"Tomorrow, you go to your first battle, for which you have waited with such patience."

There was laughter here, for it was common knowledge that the men had been in bad temper for some days, awaiting this battle.

"We have shown you how to fight in ways strange and unusual to you. Let us hope that they will be as strange to the Hygerians. You will be outnumbered here, though not so seriously as you will likely be in future battles, and the Hygerian is a fierce fighter, fearing nothing under the sun. Remember that your people on the plains depend on us to win this battle, and that if we win the battle, it will be a beginning.

"Too long now have we known the rule of a people who do not rightly know what a city is, nor a road, not a proper farm. Too long have they taken from us what they would, and left nothing but bitterness. But now shall the bitterness be many times repaid. Victory to Asbaln with Conel!"

The war-host roared out its response. By now, after many weeks of practicing theorized tactics against imaginary enemies, the burning flame of pride and anger which had driven them to the Hills to fight for Conel was beginning to wane. But the prospect of battle in the morning brought it out in a blaze.

Even the few older men among them, with good cause to know what a battle meant, were caught up by the high spirits. They gave three loud cheers for the Prince, three more for the Guardian, then went back to their quarters to prepare for the morning. As they walked back from the gathering-place just outside the village, Helana came out to meet Rorick.

"So you go to battle again tomorrow?" She tried to keep the worry from her voice and eyes.

"Aye, it is the first battle for the infantry. Few of them have any experience, but they are all good lads." Seeing her concern showing through, he said, "I have worried more about battles than this. And why should we even speak of the subject, you and I? There are more pleasant things to discuss." She smiled briefly.

They strolled across the face of the hill, quietly talking of this and that. He was half-listening to her, watching the light evening breeze ruffle her long brown hair, when something loomed over the crest of the hill. He turned, reaching for the Sword, and saw a troll coming at them. At the same moment, another troll came round the side of the hill toward them.

He shouted at Helana, "Go on, get back to the village!" One man might fight a troll, but two were too many. She turned to run, but caught her foot in a loop of root and fell.

Rorick sidestepped a rush from the first troll, noticing as he did so that this troll was smaller than the first one he had fought. He chopped into the beast's leg and turned to meet the second one. The second troll was no larger than his comrade, but still larger than Rorick. He sprang, arms spread.

Rorick went down on one knee, thrusting up and forward with the Sword. In that same instant, the glow of the Sword heightened to a flaring brilliance, then disappeared. The beast impaled itself on the blade, and Rorick rolled aside as the troll fell where he had been. With a jerk, he brought the Sword free.

In the instant of time he had before he must turn to his other opponent, it seemed to him that the dead troll's face had relaxed into an expression of long-sought peace. The first troll's injured leg was fully healed now, and he came forward in a series of little feinting hops, apparently trying to make Rorick swing with the Sword and open himself to the troll's attack.

Then, without warning, the green monster stepped in fast and swung a huge fist. Rorick ducked under the troll, thrusting upward with the Sword. Again came the flaring brilliance, swiftly fading, and the Sword thrust home. Even as it did, the troll was swinging its other arm. Rorick tried to dodge, but it caught him glancingly on the side of the head, and he fell beside the dead troll.

By now Helana had freed herself from the grasping root, and fearfully approached Rorick. She found him alive, but unconscious. Quickly, she went into the village to get help in bringing him back. When they carried him back, they found that his hand would not relax its grip on the Sword, so that they had to carry both back together. In spite of the fears of some, he soon recovered, and went out to walk among them to stop any rumours that he was injured, dead, or dying.

Chapter Eight

How was the Kingdom of Avantir saved from destruction during the first harsh years of its existence? One of the reasons was the ancient bond between the Guardians of the Sword and the People of the Hills. Barbarian tribes seeking to invade Avantir out of the Wild Lands must either fight their way through the Icarian Hills, or swing wide round to cross the River. In either case, the men of Avantir had adequate warning, and Darkon's companions were always ready to meet them. Never did the Hill People forget that ancient link with the Guardians.

—Avantir, the Kingdom Out of the Ruins Ammerlyn

The story set the camp abuzz. It was unheard of for a man to kill two trolls, a deed worthy of the Elder Hero Garthell Long-sword, or the more recent Karkal of the Silver Ring. There was not a man among the war-host but wished to prove himself worthy of such a leader.

The leaders spent some time in the making of plans for the battle. Rorick looked at Beran. "The Infantry accept you as their commander?"

"Well enough, I suppose. Some might think it better to have a man of birth and position to lead them, but most will take their orders from me. And we have very few men of birth and position left, have we?"

"So be it. If all goes well, we shall march against Virdan within the week."

IN THE MORNING, Rorick, Conel, and Randell, who commanded the cavalry, along with Beran and the three other commanders of the infantry, sat talking in the Chief's house. They had just laid out the plan for the battle with daggers and drinking—cups, and Rorick had answered some last minute questions about tactics.

But Rorick knew, beyond question, that the real test would be when the commanders were required to improvise to meet some Hygerian action not allowed for in the plans.

A man came in, wearing a slightly large Hygerian chain—shirt, a Hygerian helmet with the spike a little clumsily removed, and a shield with a rather carefully painted Red Dragon on the face.

"The host is ready, Lords and Captains."

The infantry, who must be in position first, donned helmets and tightened armour—buckles, then went out. Helana entered, and poured for the three remained a cup each of the Hill—peoples' ale, the secret of which is not divulged to strangers at any price.

"Fortune favour you, Conel, rightful King of Asbaln. Randell, son of my mother's brother, *Khabarstymbion*, may you return in safety. For you, Rorick, what words are left? I will wait for you, as long as I must."

"So long as the Sword serves me, I shall return to you."

But then it was time for the Horsemen to leave, and they took up their gear, striding out into the sunlight. The wolf—shaggy, laughing—eyed Horsemen waited outside, standing, sitting, or squatting in the dust, idly tossing knucklebones. As the Commanders stepped out, they were up and adjusting harnesses, donning helmets, and mounting. Conel gave the order to march, and as they rode out, Rorick turned to catch a glimpse of Helana in the door—way of the Chief's house.

As they neared the place where they planned to fight the Hygerians, Rorick turned to Conel and said,

"Now we go to battle;

For the freedom of our land;

But one prize do I desire;

A fair brown maiden's hand."

Conel stared off across the horizon for a moment, then answered,

"I sing a song of evil times, of armies lost and fled,

Of hunted King in Hidden Hills, no crown upon his head;

I sing a song of victory, of triumph in the land,

A King who rides to gain his crown, a friend at either hand."

Then Randell spoke as well,

"A battle is a chancy thing, be it lost or won;

And fleeting are affairs of men who walk beneath the sun.

Kingdoms rise and kingdoms fall, and one thing still is sure

When empires all are gone to dust, yet will the earth endure."

The Hygerians marched along the same route as their previous party. About four hundred infantry and a little more than two hundred cavalry came up, and fell into order against the five hundred Asbalnian infantry and the hundred and twenty Horsemen who supported them. The Hygerian cavalry took up positions on either end of the line, preventing the Asbalnians from circling the infantry. These were matched on the Asbalnian side by two small groups of cavalry at each end of the infantry line, while Rorick sat in the rear with another small group of cavalry.

As planned, Conel and Randell led out their cavalry wings to keep the Hygerians occupied. They avoided coming to close quarters, but rather led the Hygerians to chase them. The Hygerians carried javelins, but the Horsemen tried to stay out of range.

Then the Asbalnian infantry opened ranks to let Rorick and his squadron through. They rode up close to the Hygerians, so close that a few javelins landed among them, and loosed arrows, then rode back again. About two horse—lengths from their own lines, they turned to ride back again e This time they went in even closer, launching their arrows into the dark—clad ranks.

This time, just as he launched his arrow, Rorick felt his horse stagger, then looked down to see that the beast had taken a javelin in the chest. Dying, the horse ignored the guiding pressure of Rorick's knees and ran on toward the enemy. Without warning, he fell forward, casting the Guardian over his head.

Rorick had already let go his bow and had a close enough grip on his shield that he could hold on to it in spite of being flung head over heels. He came to his feet about five close paces from the Hygerian ranks.

In the instant he had to make up his mind, he realized that to flee would mean taking a javelin in the back inside five paces, whereas to attack into their ranks would mean doing some little damage before he died. He stepped forward.

A JAVELIN WENT glancingly off his shield. An arrow sang away from his helmet. Then he was in range. He took one spear—thrust on his shield, warded another with the Sword, stepped forward between them, and struck. An instant later, he was through the spearmen in front and into the archers and javelin—throwers behind. Hygerian archers and javelin—men wear light armour and carry no shields, so he was able to down two before they could draw swords. Then they surrounded him.

Suddenly, behind him, he heard more shouting and battle—noise, and as he moved with all possible speed to keep the enemy back, Beran burst through the Hygerian line at the head of a wedge of twenty men. Then Beran was beside the Guardian, and the Hygerians were falling back from the ferocity of their attack.

"We have come in time, then, Milord?"

"Just in time, my old friend."

"Aye. The men fight well, do they not? But we must leave here." He shouted some orders, and they withdrew foot by foot until they were back outside the Hygerian lines. The main force of Asbalnian infantry were by this time in battle with the Hygerian front line.

By now as well, the Hygerian cavalry had been drawn far enough from the infantry to allow the rest of Rorick' s squadron, under the capable leadership of his second in command, to sweep around the rear. This, coupled with the steadiness of the infantry, caused the Hygerians to break and ran. Rorick, Conel, and Randell's second in command held them back from pursuit.

Among the twenty—two Icarians and forty—eight infantry dead was Randell. In the second attack, he had gone down with a Hygerian javelin in the chest.

Chapter Nine

No wooden wall, be it built sky—tall,
Shall help them keep my lady.
O Powers above, watch the one that I love, For they shall not keep my lady.
I ride this day, and tonight I slay, But they shall not keep my lady;
With the Sword in hand I must make a stand, For I ride to take my *lady.*
Let the host not bide, but following ride to meet me and my lady.
When evening falls, so shall their walls,
For they took away my lady.
—from "The Rescue of Helana" Conel of Asbaln.

They camped the war—host some ways from the battlefield, in the direction of the lowlands. Conel and Rorick rode back to Carill Don to make final arrangements and found that all events of that day had not been equally favourable.

A small band of Hygerian cavalry, led by an Icarian traitor, had raided the village. Apparently, the Icarian had been able to lead them by hidden pathways so that their approach remained unmarked, and to be sure, the most attention had been on the main body of Hygerians, with little to spare for other possibilities.

They had had a particular plan in mind, for they had gone directly to Chief Orn's house. He had not been in, but they had taken Helana, and before the Chief could organize more than twenty men to fight, the raiders had gone.

The Icarian traitor had not escaped; he had already been burned, his bow and quiver with him, and his name forbidden.

The raiders would be going back to Virdan, and with the news of this morning's battle, they would most certainly not risk moving so important a prisoner over the open roads until they could see what effect this would have on the people. At the very least, they would mere arrangements for a very large escort, which again the commander of the fort would be loath to grant immediately on the news of the defeat of their any in the Hills.

Orn met with Conel and Rorick. "They would use her to make me cease giving aid to your cause."

"We will understand that, Chief. You have done much already in giving us shelter and food."

"*They* do not understand!" The Chief's eyes flared, "I will not trade our honour, even for the life of my only daughter. If it must be so, she shall die, even as Randell died. *Kr yrriech.*"

The war—cry of the Derrakos of the Swamp, which was the war—cry of the Icarians as well, expressed the final fatalistic statement on unavoidable fate. Whatever else might happen, the Earth endures. The Earth only endures, so should men expect eternal existence?

"I will rescue her alive."

Conel and Orn both looked at Rorick. "How will you do that? When the war—host, or any sizeable body of men appears outside Virdan, they will show her on the walls and ask the Icarians among us how they value her. And if we attack, she will die."

"Ah, Conel, but if I go alone, and by night? I would wager that I could make my way into the fort unseen."

"You would wager your life if you lose. Or do you possess a cape of invisibility? I must forbid it, Rorick; we cannot spare you."

"On the contrary, if I should die in attempting Virdan, will you not have an army enraged, bent on destroying it log by log? But I will not fail, nor will I consent to let the matter pass."

Conel looked deeply into his eyes. After a moment, he nodded. "So be it, then. Ride when you are ready, and will bring up the war—host as quickly as might be. You will have this night in which to accomplish your purpose, for we will have the men in front of Virdan by noon tomorrow."

"So be it. I shall take a moment for food, get a fresh horse, if one is to be found, and be gone."

Rorick was just eating hastily when the Old One came to him, chagrin showing in his face. "It was in the message. I had only just solved the riddle of the writing and was bringing my result to the Chief when the attack came. I regret I was not swift enough to prevent this."

"Things happen."

"Yes. But perhaps I can do something to make up for it. You are no magician, I perceive, yet no doubt you have used minor spells, lock—spells and the like?"

"I have." Rorick regarded the magician with curiosity.

"Good. I have a spell which may be of use to you. It will increase your physical strength for a short period of time, something which you may need."

"It would be useful indeed."

"Good. This is a spell requiring an aspect of concentration, and for your purposes, I would suggest that you use the Sword. Put your hand on it, and say these words."

For a few minutes, he rehearsed Rorick carefully in a short phrase in a strange language. At last, he was satisfied with Rorick's recitation. The Guardian mounted up, and as he prepared to ride out, Conel approached him.

"I cannot like this, but I can see how you would feel it must be done. May the High Powers smile upon you and your lady."

"And on you also, Conel."

He waited, some distance from the fort, for the sun to disappear completely, and for thick darkness to spread over all. He then slowly and carefully led his horse down to the nearest clump of brush to the fort, then lay down on the ground, his dark—red war—cloak spread over him. In that light, he would resemble only another hummock on the ground, and any guards would be looking for whole armies, not single men creeping up on them.

Even without light to show him, it took him a long time to cross that space, but finally he was there. Above him, a sentry was silhouetted against the sky. He moved down a little, about the middle of the five—yard interval between sentries, and took out the length of rope he had brought along, with a loop knotted in it.

When both sentries were looking away, he threw the loop upward to settle softly over one of the posts. The rasping sound as he pulled it tight sounded loud enough to wake the whole garrison, but neither of the sentries paid any notice to it.

Softly, with his hand on the Sword, he spoke the words of the spell of strength. Then, as both the sentries had looked away once again, he went up the rope fast. Holding to the edge of the wall, he dropped his dagger onto the catwalk inside. This time, the noise was clearly audible to both sentries. He hung there by his arms until one of them came over to investigate; when the man bent over, mystified, to pick up the dagger, Rorick pulled himself up to deliver a hard blow to the back of the man's neck with the bottom edge of his right fist.

As the Hygerian clattered limply to the catwalk, Rorick came over in a quick movement. The other sentry brought up his javelin for the cast; swept up the fallen sentry's spear and threw it underhanded. The Hygerian's javelin whipped past his head. The javelin he had thrown hit the man in the chest, and he fell limply from the walk.

He looked around. Through some sort of blind luck, none of the other nearby sentries had paid any mind to the proceedings. There would clearly not be much time, though. He went to the nearest stair and met a man coming up. Without hesitation, he kicked the Hygerian in the chest, and the black–clad warrior new backward off the stair. He still had not moved when Rorick went by at a run to the prison building.

He stopped in front of the thick wooden door and kicked it three times with his heel. On the second blow it cracked, on the third, half swung inward on the hinges, half hung awkwardly from the look for a moment, then fell. He stepped inside. Helana was there, chained to the wall by her right ankle, and three other men, one a mere boy, one so old and shrunken as to make a person wonder how he could possibly have offended the Dark ones.

Helana recognized him even in the dimness. “Rorick! But I heard no sound of battle.”

“Nor will you, if we leave here quickly enough. I came alone to bring you out safely before we attack.” He turned to the other men. “What would you? I can set you free, and you can take your risks outside if they hunt us, or you can wait until we take the fortress. You have nearly no time at all to decide.”

He raised the Sword and brought it down in a swift and powerful blow against the chain on Helana’s ankle. The chain parted easily, and the Guardian looked round at the other three. The man nodded. “I will come, Lord. And if it be possible, Aln, son of Arin, will be with your host when you attack these walls.”

The boy swallowed, tried to speak, swallowed again and said, “I am Jeric Torbin’s ward, and I will not stay here longer than I must.”

“So be it.” In two quick strokes, Rorick freed the two. The older men looked up at him.

“I don’t be so young as I were, Lord, I run not so fast, I climb not so well. Be’t your pleasure, I will wait for you and all your armies to come.”

Rorick nodded. “Had you asked my advice, that would have been it. The rest of you, come.”

As they stepped outside, they heard the alarm being given from the wall.

“So it goes. We will be at a run now, and I will lead you to the rope I have left hanging on the wall. If you have the opportunity, you might pick up weapons from some of the dead, for you might see them useful.”

Four men met them coming down the stair as they went up. Only one could pass at a time, and Rorick engaged them fiercely with the Sword. The first went down with the Guardian’s first swing; the second, his blow parried, took a thrust which felled him; the third caught a sword—swing on his shield, but Rorick’s added strength drove him sidewise off the stair. Finally, the fourth, several steps back, was raising a javelin to throw.

Rorick, without a shield, knew himself doomed, but leaped up the steps, determined to die trying. Something flew past his head from behind, ringing sharply against the Hygerian’s armour. Rorick saw the Hygerian dagger falling away, then the javelin went past him, surprise causing the Hygerian's cast to go awry. By then, the Guardian was close enough to strike with the Sword, and when he had dispatched the enemy, he looked around. Helana was holding a second Hygerian dagger, ready to throw.

Behind her, Aln, son of Arin, held a Hygerian sword and looked somewhat disgruntled. "I would have come behind you, Lord, but she moves uncommonly quick."

Rorick grinned. "We must all move uncommon quick. Come on."

On the catwalk, they went swiftly to the rope, which was still hanging where he had left it. Ten Hygerians were rushing up the stairs, several more were coming from each side. Helana went over the wall and down the rope; Jeric Torbin's ward leaned over, dropped two javelins down, and went scrambling down himself. Aln stood back to back with Rorick against the first fierce rush of Hygerian, and when they drew back for a moment, Rorick said, "Go now, hurry!"

"What of you, Lord?"

"I shall come. I will do better as rear—guard than you, for I have my mail—shirt. Go!"

With a nod, Aln went over the wall and down the rope. The Hygerians moved in again, but Rorick backed against the wall and fought fiercely. He reached behind him, pulled up a length of the rope, and gripped it firmly in his left hand. For a moment, the Hygerians drew back again, and in that moment the Guardian leaped over the wall, holding fast to the rope.

With a shout to those below, he dropped the Sword and swarmed down the rope, dropping the last two feet as someone above slashed through the rope. A Hygerian, black cloak flapping, fell from the wall to land beside him, and Rorick saw the javelin protruding from his chest. He turned. Aln and Helana were beside him. Jeric stood a few yards out from the wall, his arm extended with the cast of his second javelin.

"Run now! For the brush!"

Several javelins hissed past them as they ran, but a stationary target silhouetted against a night sky is a different matter from moving figures on the ground, aimed at from above. When they reached Rorick's horse, they stopped. Rorick looked around at the little group. "Aln, Jeric, here we must part. They will hunt the hardest for myself and the lady, so if you are able to find a place to hide, you will see little more danger this night. I owe you both much; if you come to me after, I will do what may for you."

"We owe you our freedom, Lord. But there is little time for chattering here. Jeric, lad, let us find a place to hide. In the morning, you can tell me how you leaned to fling a javelin so well."

The Guardian helped Helana up onto the horse, then urged him along into a run, trotting along beside. "I am sorry, heart—of—mine, but even for you I could not risk another of our horses. I will run beside you for a while."

A hasty back-ward glance shoved a few Hygerians coming out of the fort on horseback at a canter, breaking into a run as they passed the gate. Starlight winked on armour and weapons. He was able to run beside the horse for only a little while, even with his augmented strength, and soon found it necessary to swing up to the horse behind Helana.

"We have a small lead, but they will catch us in the long run. We must reach the war—host before the Dark ones reach us."

They topped a rise, and far, far back he heard a shout as the pursuers sighted them. "I wish I *had* risked another horse."

"If wishes were arrows, what trade would fletchers follow?" said Helana, quoting an old Hill saying.

The horse flew through the darkness, over the rough trail. Rorick silently prayed to the High Ones that the horse's hooves might not find a hole or obstruction. He decided that when the pursuers came too close, he would dismount and delay them as best he could.

As he thought about it, he decided it was probably due to the effectiveness of the Horsemen that the Hygerians were likely to run them down. The existence of a band of mounted archers had probably caused them to keep a small force of cavalry at arms at all times, so that when the alarm was raised, all that was needful was for them to throw saddles on their horses and be away.

He considered turning aside from the main trail, riding for one of the close by stands of wood and attempting to lose his pursuers. It seemed, however, that off the trail the chances were better of having his horse fall or be lamed. Best to continue as they were and hope for something better. He knew of a place or two, where, if necessary, he might take refuge among some rocks. With his bow and a handful of arrows from the saddle—quiver, he could guarantee to keep the Hygerians at bay for a time, perhaps even long enough for some of Conel's scouts to reach them.

But this was all profitless speculation if the Hygerians continue to overtake them at the present rate. He leaned over to Helana. "My lady, take the horse and ride on if I dismount."

She turned a little to address him. "Why should you die and I live?"

"So that my death should be for something. No, I do not leave you yet, for there remains some small chance. But when I do, you must go on."

She made no answer, but he could feel her dislike for the eventuality. On they went. Suddenly, mounting a small rise, they saw mounted figures ahead in the dimness. Determined that the enemy should not have an easy time in taking them, he drew the Sword.

As it gleamed free with its own inner light, he heard cries from those before him, and realized just in time that they were shouting "Victory for Asbaln with Conel!" He drew up his horse, but the speed at which he was travelling made it necessary for him to go past them, and as he turned, he saw them loose their arrows.

It was no light for any sort of shooting, but the Hygerians were too few to wish to face any number of mounted archers, and allowed themselves to be easily discouraged. The leader of the party of Horsemen was a stocky little man, looking like a barrel on horseback, and he grinned a ferocious little grin.

"We've a camp up this way a few more miles. The King sent us out to guide you in. And may say for us all that we are glad to see you whole?"

Chapter Ten

Death to the enemies of the King!
Dark ones, hear our wild swords sing!
Death to the dark-haired western men!
Death from Foothill, Plain, and Fen!
Down with Virdan's wooden walls!
See now, how the fortress falls!
Swiftly, through the broken gate!
Now they rally, but too late.
Hunt them now, over hill and plain!
Bright swords strike and strike again;
Arrows flash in the morning sun;
Fiercely now is the battle done.
-from "Battle of Virdan"
Artir One-eye of the Midland Plain

Rorick discovered that Orn's answer to the taking of Helana had been to encourage the Icarians to join Conel, giving him a force of one hundred picked Icarian archers. They had managed to gather enough lost Hygerian horses to mount a hundred and thirty Horsemen, while the infantry force numbered five hundred. Altogether, they were about equal to the garrison in Virdan, which meant, ordinarily, that they had not much chance of winning.

Between then, however, they arranged a plan which they thought might be successful. One of its major features was the fact that they were descending on Virdan somewhat sooner than anyone expected them to.

As they moved down over the last slope toward the fortress, Conel spoke. "We are here at last. I had always disliked the idea of allowing them to build this fortress. It has made our provisioning and recruitment difficult."

"Yet I think you will be as glad that we allowed ourselves the extra time for training. Had we had fewer men in the Hills, I would have had to agree with you and stop the building of the fortress. But now we are here, and we have come to the plains to stay."

Before they attacked, they sent into the fort, wrapped around an Icarian arrow, a message demanding that the occupants surrender in the name of Conel, heir to the throne of Asbaln.

They received an answer, on the shaft of a Hygerian javelin, demanding that they surrender in the none of Razak, King of the Hygerians, Destined Conqueror, Shepherd of the People.

Rorick appraised the army. It was the same tatterdemalion force, larger now, a little more variously armed, but all determined to fight. "We shall see a battle here today," he told Conel.

"Whatever else one might say about the Hygerians, they are no cowards."

"True words, Rorick, my friend. But here are the Horsemen with the ram." He tuned and called a word of command, and a trumpeter sounded his horn:

"The swords of old Asbaln lay long in the dust,

The shield of my father is crumbled to rust;

From my haunt in the hills I have come to the plain;

Now what Dryx Field did forfeit, let Virdan regain."

Rorick answered:

"The time of the axe and the sword is upon us,

Above us the storm-clouds fly;

Woe to the widows and woe to the orphans,

For husbands and lovers will die."

During that morning's march, the Horsemen had taken time to cut down and trim a medium-sized tree and fit six pairs of stout rope handles to it. A group of them now went forward, bearing it between them, while Icarian archers stood ready to prevent any Hygerian from casting a missile at them with impunity. Some of the Horsemen held up shields to cover those bearing the ram.

For a little, the ram swung with no apparent effect except for a booming noise. Some of the Hygerians took the risk of appearing momentarily above the gate to cast javelins down, and most died for their pains. Some simply cast javelins and other missiles down by reaching above the wall with their arms, but three of the Horsemen were downed by missiles, two killed.

Then the gate creaked. Two blows later, it cracked. On the next blow, the great bar inside pulled from the wall with a crash and the gate flew open. Without hesitation, the Horsemen rode in to prevent it being closed again, and Rorick, now afoot, led in the infantry on their heels. The Guardian and the infantry advanced steadily forward in line until a wild, rushing band of Hygerians threw themselves forward to break it.

They succeeded, sacrificing their lives in the deed, shouting "*Washariba ghelhagir!* We do it for the families!"

Behind them came more, in a steadier fashion, to take advantage of the disruption.

For a time, the Guardian was isolated and surrounded. But Sword, shield, and armour served him well until the second line of Asbaln's infantry had forced its way to where he stood. That was the barbarian's last effort to win the battle.

Some twenty fought their way out and flee, about thirty surrendered, mostly through being too badly wounded to continue fighting, but the rest fought and died where they stood.

The Asbalnians were elated with two victories in as many days, but Rorick and Conel both knew that it was surprise as much as anything which had allowed them to take Virdan. Indeed, it must not be forgotten that the Hygerians were fully unused to holding fortresses of any sort.

THEY REPAIRED THE GATE of the fortress, and established themselves in the neighbourhood, then called on the people to come to them. In the meantime, they sent out their forces in all directions to deal with all the lesser garrisons between the Mountains and the River. Rorick and Conel had personally led several of these minor forays, but most of their time was spent in the gathering of an army. Still, strangely, no Hygerian force took the field against them.

Swift as the very Birds of Brhandon, the word went from village to village, from farm to farm:

"Conel rides forth,

The Red Dragon is raised,

The Sword is Not to be Named,

Has been unsheathed."

Plans were made for the next attack, that against the walled City of Orden. It was built entirely of good stone, and save for Avantir, was the only strong Hygerian fortress east of the Mountains. Recruitment and training went on, and they now found themselves less pressed for decent horses, a situation which they did not expect to see continue for long.

They set to work quickly at training their new men, using some of the very best of those who had come down out of the Hills for the purpose of teaching. They did not expect to wait until the new men were fully as well trained as the old, but intended that they should be given as much training as possible. When the time came, they would be divided up and placed among those whom they smilingly referred to as 'veterans.'

Five days after the battle for Virdan, something important happened. Conel and Rorick, late in the afternoon, were talking matters of strategy in one of many tents which had been pitched outside the fort to accommodate those of Asbaln's war-host for whom there was not enough room within the walls. Suddenly, they heard a minor commotion outside. Rising, they saw five men riding into the camp.

The leader was a large man going fat, and quite old. His white hair and beard surrounded a wrinkled, weathered face. He wore a war-shirt, a leather jacket with several metal plates sewn upon it, and his war-cap was leather, bound with three metal bends. His sword seemed a large one, the hilt wooden, once broken, but mended neatly and efficiently with wire. On the scabbard was some writing, done in silver threads, though some of the original threads had gone missing, and had been replaced with ordinary white thread. But most interesting was the fact that the letters were of Cymruthair, the Kingdom of the Elder Folk, which few Mortal Men could read.

A few among the host who claimed some acquaintance with these letters declared they read there the name of Thumill the Lucky, Thumill of the Three Rings, the Hero. This news went through the army of Asbaln like a wind through standing wheat, a sustained whisper.

Yet more to the immediate point was the fact that the four young men with him, obviously his sons, were armed as well. It was seen that he bore a shield slung at his saddle, round, made of wood, with a metal rim and a metal boss. His eldest son had a copy of that shield, without the metal, and a sword. One other had an axe, and a cap made of leather, folded several times and boiled to harden it. One had a bow and arrows, and a longish bronze dagger, clearly the workmanship of the barbarians of the Wild Lands. The last bore only a six-foot spear, and wore a cloth cap with a feather in it.

All eyes turned to this last and remained a moment, for he was slighter and darker of complexion than the others, with thin, almost feminine features, strange in the light of the broad blonde handsomeness of the rest of the family.

As the father swung down from his saddle, the others also dismounted, simultaneously, as though it were a thing they had practised. The father tossed his reins to the son with the wooden shield, then strode to the group before the tent. After running his eye quickly over then, he spoke.

"You'd be the king," he stated, looking at Conel, "And you'd be the Guardian of the Sword." He glared at Rorick. "Now, Lords, begging your pardon, but could you show some proof? You see, we were hearing of rumours about men in the Hills, with names being given, and some of those names of men I know to be dead these five years on Dryx field. I am not saying that as one part of a story is known untrue that the rest must also be lies, but I am wishing to be sure.

"But now you're here, and you've been successful enough in what you've done, so men will approach you, and if you be not what you say you are, those who be coming may suddenly be finding themselves lost. It may not seem heroic, but I'm having a strong desire to be knowing who and what I fighting for."

Rorick smiled. "I recognize your feelings, and I sympathize. Here is my proof." The Sword came free of its scabbard. "Here shines the Sword Which is Not to Be Named, and with it will I do all in my power to deliver and defend Asbaln from her foes. And by this blade do I swear that the man beside me is Conel, rightful King of Asbaln, and my sworn Lord. Will that suffice?"

"For yourself, it will, for I am knowing the look of the Sword, and I am thinking that no man might be swearing a false oath on it without woe. Yet for the look of it, at the least, I would have the King speak for himself."

Conel shrugged. "I am Conel, son of Gunn, of the line of Conel the Wild. No more proof have I save that those here follow me, believing me to be who I claim to be."

The old farmer nodded. "You are either the King, or one who will serve as well. I am Cadda, son of Fannan, son of Brenan, son of Fernmal. These are my sons, Fannan, Vandinal, Dannan, and Brioghir. We'll be joining your host, with the exception of Brioghir, who must stay with the farm." The youngest began a protesting motion with his hands, but subsided.

"You're the youngest, Brioghir, and perhaps the best able to care for the farm. Tell the neighbours, tell them we've seen the King, and we'll be going with him."

Brioghir swung to his horse, saluted the King and his father, then rode away. Cadda looked at the King and said, "He'll see to it the neighbours know. He's a good lad."

The Old One stood by, leaning on a staff. "You call him Brioghir. Is that not a Tyuridan name?"

Cadda nodded. "His mother named him so. She came from Tyurid, after some sort of strife and feud there. She spoke of being of the vigh-Hohech clan."

"Indeed?" The Old One's eyebrows rose expressively. "I must speak to you again, Cadda. But I am delaying the King and the Guardian."

Cadda was passed on to one of the infantry captains, and the two leaders of the host went back to their plans..

DURING ALL THE TIME that they remained around Virdan, they had had scouts in pairs and in small parties out to watch Orden and all the area between. It became clear that the Hygerians were not planning on sending a war-host against Virdan, at least, not immediately. Rather, they were strengthening their hold on Orden, bringing in more men and supplies. Reports of casual conversations with Hygerian officers revealed that they expected that the Asbalnians would hurl themselves against the walls of Orden and be destroyed there.

There were now more than a thousand men in Orden, with more always arriving, and food was stored for half a year. The men of Asbaln did not have that much time. Orden must fall swiftly, and the King must have possession of at least the whole of the Midland Plain by winter.

The Old One was assisting them in the production of large machines, capable of throwing arrows or small stones for great distances, as well as larger engines, with which stones of great size might be thrown against city walls or gates. With these, it was hoped that they could take Orden swiftly, before a Hygerian force could fall upon them camped at the city walls.

Three weeks after the fall of Virdan, they went to Orden. One morning, the barbarians in the city looked out to see an Asbalnian army of over a thousand men outside.

Chapter Eleven

So far as is known, Rorick is the first of the Guardians to make use of the greater powers of the Sword, though there are some rumours and fragmentary ballads regarding Arvandal. it is said that the Sword cares for its Wielder, and when the necessity for any of the Sword's powers arises, it will give to its Wielder the necessary knowledge for their use. There are some who say that these powers and their nature prove the Sword is the master and its Wielder, but a puppet. However, none of the Guardians have ever expressed an opinion on the subject.

-Book of the Sword
Kerran Berandis

A man came into the Asbalnian camp that morning, walking from the south. The man was tall and blonde, square-featured, and he smiled seldomly. He dressed like a free-warrior, with a chain war-shirt and helmet. He carried no shield, but thrust through the red and blue sash at his waist were two short swords of Dwarfish make.

The camp guards brought him to the Prince and the Guardian, as he asked, and when he was there, he told them, "I am called Donal the Bane, sometimes Donal Two-Sword, and I am from a land far away. I was brought here by a spell, and by a spell I am required to bring some special news to your chief magician. When I have discharged that obligation, I ask to be allowed to fight in whatever battle shall happen today."

The Old one stepped forward, extended a finger, and spoke:

"Shalak deflun rodosekh

Trilekh flonha tirelekh!"

A sudden flare of light burst forth between the two, and as Asbaln's men fell back in wonderment, the old magician and the young warrior regarded each other. Donal smiled grimly. "Aye, old one, speak the truth, and I have a magic of my own. But have you a spell of the Arkh-bazd Whazar unearthed from some moldering book which will tell you what my news is?"

The Old One bowed to Conel and Rorick, then took the young man off to his tent to speak. The rest of the host formed up in battle array. By this time, the Hygerians had seen the small size of the Asbalnian force and tested them. Two-hundred cavalry trotted out the main gate, accompanied by five hundred infantry. The cavalry, due to some wild whim of the man commanding them, did not stay with the infantry to cooperate with them, but dashed out in a mad charge toward the King's Horsemen.

The King's Horsemen had a new style of fighting, tested so far in small patrol actions, now meeting its first major trial. Each man, besides his bow, arrows, and sword, bore a twelve-foot lance slung across his back. Each man also had a small round shield slung at his saddle, balancing the bow case, as it were.

Seeing the direction of the cavalry advance, they moved forward themselves, shooting as they came. At what they felt to be a safe enough distance, they slung their bows at their saddles, took up the shields, unslung their spears, and charged. The shields were small, smaller than many felt comfortable with, but it was necessary to have shields which could be handled swiftly and easily. It was to be hoped their manoeuvrability would make up somewhat for their size.

The bows of the Horsemen did dreadful work among the Hygerians, and the long lances completed their work. Many of the Hygerians did not even attempt to come to grips with the advancing foe, even those who were themselves equipped with lances, and of the two hundred who rode forth, only seventy-five returned to the gate of the city.

In the meantime, three hundred infantry were advancing to meet the Hygerian foot, with fifty Icarians behind them, loosing arrows over their heads. The arrows influenced morale, though the Hygerians managed some sort of answer at close range with their javelins. Then, with a ringing crash, the two lines came together. For a moment, there was no movement. Then, it appeared the Hygerians fell back a trifle. Then it was sure that they had, and were still falling back, for behind the firm Asbalnian line were black-cloaked corpses.

Suddenly the Horsemen, having conclusively driven off the Hygerian cavalry, returned to strike into the rear of the infantry. In a moment, the remainder of that original band of five hundred were running, in ones, twos, and little bands, for the gate. But one group, fifty strong, formed a circled and retired slowly and steadily toward the gate, presenting a snarling front of fury toward any attackers. They used javelins as thrusting spears to keep off cavalry. They retired before the infantry and they suffered the arrows, but they continued on, and forty of them reached the gates, whereas those merely fled were cut down from behind. There were over two hundred Hygerian dead on the field when the gate was closed.

Rorick looked at Conel. "If they take that little band and use them as officers to train the rest of their infantry, they would destroy us."

"True. Though I would have preferred seeing all of them dead on the field, I must say that I feel a strong admiration for them They did not panic, they did not trust to their feet to save them, they knew they must be prepared to fight whatever came if they would escape. And they escaped."

"Our only consolation is they have not yet shown any desire to make their foot an arm of respectable worth. I will say they improve, but they seem to be more concerned with the use of their horse. Then, too, we *should* intend that none of these men escape to train anyone."

By this time, the Horsemen were amusing themselves by riding near the walls and shooting at any Hygerian who dared to show himself. The catapults were being finally positioned, and the huge one facing the main gate was being supplied with half-ton boulders. Suddenly a man appeared on the wall, in flowing black robes, guarded by two warriors who stood on either side of him with large shields. He pointed a finger and shouted a word which shuddered in the air. There was a screaming hiss as a large fireball flew forth, growing in size until it struck down a Horseman, burning horse and all into a lump of cinder.

Again came the word, and again a ball of screaming orange fire smote a horse and rider. By the time of the third fireball, all the Horsemen were riding away from the walls with all alacrity.

Rorick rode to a catapult, meeting the crew as they abandoned it. He blocked the path of their retreat, and when they looked up into his face, they hesitated only a moment before returning to the machine and moving it to aim at the warlock on the wall.

Perhaps, as some claimed, he could divine the thoughts of men, and perhaps he simply looked to those places where men remained at their posts below him. In any case, the next ball of fire struck the catapult. Rorick found himself riding forward, Sword across his saddle, past the charred ruin where the last fireball had struck. He saw the finger point at him, and heard the word pronounced.

Then he was holding the Sword up in his right hand, and the screaming ball of fire arrived. He felt only a little warmth as it disappeared in the instant of touching the Sword. Again, a fireball flew, and again it disappeared. He was aware of a tingling feeling in the hilt of the Sword, but no unpleasant sensation. A third ball struck, with no other effect. Rorick wondered if there might be a way to strike back.

Then, from the ruby in the pommel of the Sword, a beam of crimson struck. It first smote down the warlock on the wall, leaving him not even time to cry out, and without touching his shield-bearers. It played swiftly over a section of the wall, and wherever it touched, the stone turned to a white and crumbling powder. Suddenly, as it had come, the ray died away, and even as it did, ten yards of the wall where the ray had touched fell in a heap.

Rorick rode back. Conel had rallied the Horsemen, had prevented them, the Powers alone knew how, from riding with all speed back to the Hills, and had steadied the rest of the war-host. The Guardian rode to the infantry and found Beran. The rest of the band who had been his Warriors were each leaders of small groups of men among the infantry.

He called to them. "You who have served as Warriors of the Guardian. I require two hundred men, swiftly, to take through that breach in the wall. Let each of you find me twenty men, all volunteers, by the time I return."

He rode back to Conel. "What did you do?" asked the Prince.

"What strange power is that you bear?"

"I know nothing about it, gave that it came when it was needed, it performed the deed for which it came, and it is gone now. May have your permission to take two hundred men inside, perhaps to open the gates, perhaps only to hold the area around the breach so that the rest may come up?"

"Permission? Rorick, you need not ask my permission for such a foray. Merely see to it that I am informed before you leave."

At that moment, the Old One and Donal came walking out from his tent.

"Milord King, Guardian. Donal has told me strange tidings, and I will find it necessary to consider this for some time. I will say that you may trust him completely," said the Old One.

"Regarding the magician on the wall, what shall I say? None of my colleagues who are assisting me here have ever seen the like, and it appears that this man found somehow acquired a spell which acted quickly enough to be useful on a field of battle. Given time, we would have discovered its secret and destroyed its effectiveness, but the Sword has served you well."

"It has indeed. But now we go to try whether we can open the gates of Orden. This will, I think, be work for men and swords more than magic."

Donal spoke then. "Milord Guardian, may I go with you?"

Rorick looked down at the blue eyes and saw a cold bitterness.

"Will you fight at my side, then?"

Then a light shone in the eyes, and Donal spoke, "Aye, if it be your wish. I will be a shield for your right side so long as I live, Guardian."

They returned to the infantry to find them waiting patiently, formed in ranks and ready to attack. He dismounted place at their head, and Donal came up beside him. The free-warrior drew his Dwarf-swords from his sash and tossed them spinning in the air, right and left, and caught as they came down. The smile on his face held little mirth.

Rorick looked at him. "Donal, why do you fight for us, for a cause which can mean little to you?"

Donal looked at him. "There is a maid, Helnor the Fair, who lived with her uncle at an inn two days' march from the haunted forest of Tarrallalla Banarra. Because she walked with me, she lies wounded in a village near here. I have reason to hate the Hygerians."

Rorick nodded. "Will you borrow a sword and shield? I have never seen or heard of men using two small swords in such a battle as this."

Donal shot him a glance with a flash of humour in it. "Soon you shall, Milord Guardian, soon you shall."

Rorick spoke:

"Blade is swinging

Arrow flies free,

Warriors are singing

To victory."

Donal answered:

"Vengeance comes on my two swords

As into battle I go again;

Prepare, all ye Hygerian Lords,

Prepare to meet with Donal Bane."

Then Rorick raised the Sword and started for the breach. Donal was at his side as they ran, and the Icarians were loosing arrows over their heads. The Hygerians had the surprise, and a small cloud of javelins breach as the Asbalnians approached. A few fell before they reached the rubble-strewn gap, a few more fell before they crossed the barrier, but those who survived reformed, fighting, on the far side.

Donal was still at Rorick's side, and the two swords flashed and spun, becoming sword or shield at need, and few indeed struck at him twice. It was cut, thrust, parry, iron on iron, men falling at every heartbeat. The Asbalnians fought their bloody way to the gate and opened it and formed before it. Then they fought indeed!

Then Conel came through the opened gate at the head of the Horsemen, their hooves rattling and flinging sparks from the cobblestones, long lances poised. Now in the dust it became a necessity to raise war-cries, so one might distinguish friend from foe. The Asbalnians shouted "Asbaln!" or "Conel!" the Icarians cried "Kr Yrriech!" For the Hygerians, it was "*Kadwashribazd!* By our deeds!"

The Hygerians fought mainly at the gates firstly, then two hundred more Asbalnian infantry came over the breach, while Icarians took positions among the rubble and loosed careful arrows. Even so, it was a near thing, a very near thing, for the Hygerians had only to stand and hold, and they came near to doing it.

But the people of the city were forgotten. They had been in near slavery for long, and when the King's host made itself known in the Hills, those who might have led a rising were forced to give hostages for their good behaviour. Now, however, the chance of freedom seemed to be at hand, and some of them began to incite the people.

At last they came down on the Hygerians, armed with wood-axes, butchering-knives, a few swords which were kept well-hidden, along with clubs or other improvised weapons. The battle lasted until well on in the evening, among the shops and houses of the city. A few hundred of the enemy broke out and escaped, a very few surrendered, the rest fought to the death.

After the battle, Rorick discovered that, of the two hundred who had followed him into the city, a little better than one hundred fifty had survived. Donal was still beside him, and Rorick no longer doubted the efficacy of his two short swords. He had a sword-slash on the left knee, and a hole in his right arm when a Hygerian arrow had struck.

Rorick gave Beran instructions. “Gather all that remain of the two hundred who entered the city with us and keep them separate from the rest. I must go seek the Prince.”

He found Conel at last, by the breach, discussing with several people the possibility of repairing the wall immediately.

He smiled as Rorick approached. “A good fight, Rorick.”

“And an excellent charge through the gates, which put the seal to it. This leaves us but one strong fortress this side of the mountains, Avantir.”

Conel drew a deep breath. “Avantir. It will be difficult to take, near impossible. Perhaps best we simply leave them cut off from the rest of the country, leave them the choice of coming forth or starving.”

“I believe I can take the city.”

Conel raised his eyebrows, then took off his helmet and slung it at his belt, saying, “So? And I suppose you will bring down the Mountain Dwarves to delve beneath the walls, to drive a shaft into Draxon’s hall?”

Rorick smiled. “Not quite so easy, and yet easier. I will tell you precisely how only in private, for it involves a secret of Avantir I would not have known to all.”

“So, then. Let us find a place where we may be by ourselves.”

“First, I would ask a request of you.”

“If the giving of it is mine, then the gift is yours. What would you have of me, my friend?”

“A free hand to ask one hundred and fifty volunteers to be the Warriors of the Guardian, and to aid in the taking of Avantir.”

“I am thinking that you could find twice as many, with no hand from me at all. They are yours, of course, and now you must tell me how you will take Avantir from Draxon and the eight hundred and more men he has in it.”

When they had found a private place, Rorick told of the tunnel between the castle and the swamp. It was his intention to take one hundred fifty men through that tunnel, open the gates of Avantir, and hold until Conel could come through. The one hundred fifty would hardly be enough to do the task themselves, but the word was that nearly two hundred of the Guardian's Warriors had been taken with Avantir, and were still being held prisoners. If, by one means or another, they could arm these men, they could almost certainly hold the gates long enough. The critical factor would be having the war-host at the gates at the proper time.

"Aye, " said Conel, thoughtfully. "It will work if it is done well. But we will want to send troops to the pass to prevent the Hygerians from sending more men in. I think that two hundred infantry and fifty archers will be enough to hold until we are done. We will leave aside Cair Canlon, Draxon's old fortress, for there are but seventy-five men in it. How will you approach Avantir?"

"Down the river. If our presence is not reported, our surprise will be the greater. And they just might suspect something if they see a band of men moving into the swamp."

"So be it. You will enter the city ten nights from tomorrow, and at that time I will have the war-host near enough to Avantir that we, or at least some of us, can make a forced march to arrive in time to come through the gates. I think it would be best if we set up camp five or ten miles from the city; they would then be less likely to keep a close watch than with us camped all around the walls. Are you sure that you can achieve your task with so few men?"

"I had thought of it, but it will be difficult enough to bring one hundred fifty through, and try to arm the prisoners without attempting to bring in too many. And most certainly raise an alarm. No, we must do it with these, or not at all."

"So, then. When you are inside and ready, send up five flaming arrows so that we will know that it is time, and that you are waiting for us."

WHEN RORICK RETURNED to his men, he saw the Old One talking with Donal. Both Donal's wounds were bandaged, and he was talking earnestly. Though he agreed with what was being said, it was not something he liked. Seeing him, the two approached Rorick, and the Old One spoke. "Milord Guardian, with your permission, I would ask for Donal's service in a special task."

"Is he willing to go?"

"I am willing, though I do not wish to leave you, Guardian."

"What is this task which is so important?"

"Only Donal and I and one other know all the facts regarding this task, and it would be better if we do not say too much. It regards the Forest of Tarrallalla Banarra, and if the task is not done, all our battles may be in vain."

Rorick raised his eyebrows and frowned. "Does this have anything to do with the Goblins, which are said to inhabit that forest?"

"It does."

"Ah, you truly do not wish me to know much of it. Would it not perhaps be better if I were to go, using the power of the Sword?"

"Donal has more knowledge of what must be done, and he has some power of his own, which will be most important for this. And, Milord, I might be so bold as to suggest that you are needed more with the war-host."

"So be it, then. Old One, do you say that the old tales of those who haunt the forest of Tarrallalla Banarra are true?"

"Some are and some are not. Have you noticed that the name of the forest itself is not of the tongue of Asbaln? Yet I will assure you these are not the same goblins against which Garthell Long-Sword fought, for all that they jealously guard the privacy of their forest. But the only man I know who knows much of such things is Ammerlyn, the Wandering Wizard."

They went their separate ways. Then Rorick did not see Donal for some time.

RORICK APPROACHED THE tired group of men who stood and sat and gossiped in a group, with Beran watching. At his approach, they all stood attentively.

"I have come to ask you to join me, that you be Warriors of the Guardian. It is not an easy life, I promise you, and most leave the company in only one way, by death. Yet you will know that the Warriors of the Guardian are men who have the respect of all. Will you join me?"

Not a one refused the offer. They were young men, men whose pride and courage flared within them, men who would do things others would think insane, but who would give all they had, and more. And he knew, with a sudden sadness, that few of them would survive the war. He looked at Beran.

"Take them in charge, Berea. Find some paint to put the device of Avantir on their shields, for the Warriors of the Guardian are a force once more."

"It shall be done, Milord."

Chapter Twelve

The people counted the New Moons, and on the third New Moon, twenty-seven of the people were given to Tralth in the rings. And Tralth ruled over all the plain, and the Versek benefited greatly from the power of Tralth.

Then came the Baca, the Big Men, who hunted the Versek like wolves, for any time that the Versek went forth to do battle. Their small size meant that even in victory, they took terrible losses. And because the Baca bore a power as well, Tralth could give no aid to the Versek. So men of the Versek sought in all the lore and wisdom available to them, and found hints of a way of escape, a Gate to another world beyond this. Yet when Tralth became aware of it, he strove against it with all his might, until some of the Versek called on the High Powers for aid. Tralth must then content himself with sending oracles of doom and destruction.

But the people, torn between service to Tralth and survival of the people, chose survival. And it was found that Tralth, that through the nature of the Gate, could not pass through. In his final anger, Tralth arranged it so the Baca should find the route into the heart of the Versek lands, and that they should move so fast that the people had not time to escape.

But Cael, the hero, with his three hundred men, held the final barrier at the valley's mouth to let his people escape. And in the end, his force all dead on the field, Cael gave himself willingly to Tralth in exchange for his halting the Big Men for the necessary time.

And though many Versek stayed behind, the power of Tralth was lessened, for no longer were people given to him regularly. At the last, he was doomed to remain within his rings, reaching out to take whoever came near unwarily.

-Book of the Versek
*Laechan Who Stayed Behin*d

In the morning, Rorick led. his small force out northward. It would be better, he felt, if there was no possibility of the Hygerians hearing of Asbalnian warriors approaching the River, so they would go to Virdan first. There were some Icarians at Virdan, down for trading, and they showed great interest in the army's progress. Rorick, making hasty preparations for his journey, spent a good deal of time in the market square. It was there that he noticed a young Icarian woman, flanked by two young bowmen in shaggy fur kilts. Her back was to him, but he was certain he recognized her.

As he stepped up, the two men turned swiftly, hands going to their short swords, but they relaxed when they saw him. He recognized them as coming from Carill Don, though they were not men he hew personally. The woman turned then, and he saw Helana, her eyes widening with surprise. "Rorick! I thought you to be some miles south of here!"

"And I thought you to be safe in the Hills. I am on a special mission with a small force of men, and even for you, Light-in-my-heart, I will not speak of it in this market. "

"And I convinced my father it would be safe enough for me to come down here with a trading group. He asked these two, my cousins, to watch me, and asked me to enquire as to the fortunes of the army. As though he did not know why I wished to come down to Virdan."

They did not have long to spend together, and they were always under the watchful eyes of her two cousins. But Rorick, as he parted from her, kissed her and said, "I shall return to you."

"And I shall wait for you."

The Warriors went on to the River, where they set about making rafts. In two days, they had enough rafts for the whole company, and they set out. They used the current, with men manning poles solely to keep them off any obstructions in the River. Each evening they would find a fairly dry place to stop and camp, sometimes having to divide and find several places.

On the second night, as the men set up camp among the marshes, Rorick went out walking, a vague feeling of unease lying on him. When he set his hand to the hilt of the Sword, he felt a curious tingling in it, seemingly akin to the feeling he had felt when he fought the magician at Orden.

He topped a small rise and looked down into a hollow containing a ring of standing stones. They were only six feet tall, and of all which had originally made up the circle, eight remained standing. They were old, he knew, for the Derrakos made no such monuments, nor did the men of Asbaln, and these must have been set up before Asbaln's folk had come from the Old Island over the Sea on the Night of Fire.

It was only as he walked down the slope that he realized he was not entirely in control of his movements. As he strove to halt, he became aware of the strength of the power which locked his hands to his sides, and moved his legs in a slow, steady pace down the hill. He knew, somehow, he was in the grip of something which dwelt within this circle, and that once he entered that circle, he would not come out alive.

Silently, he prayed to the High Powers, striving to reach the hilt of the Sword with his left hand. Steadily, step by step, he approached the dread circle, and silently, fiercely, he strove to reach the Sword, which he somehow knew to be the only weapon he possessed against the maleficent thing which gripped him.

Then his hand twitched, jerked, and suddenly moved. He knew he had only escaped because the power in the ring was old and weak from so long without feeding. In earlier times, he would not have escaped.

As his hand found the hilt, he felt the invisible bonds disappear, and he stumbled back. As he ran for the riverbank, he felt the hilt growing unbearably hot under his hand, but he did not dare to release it until he was well away from that malevolent power.

As he stumbled back toward the camp, he shouted at the men to cease preparing camp and launch the rafts again. They looked at him in amazement, but when they saw his face, they bent to their work and were soon out in the river again.

Rorick never spoke to the men about what happened, though he asked the Old One, who told him some hints of old lore and frank tall tales. All the men claimed to have had evil dreams that night, though they moved several miles downstream.

Chapter Thirteen

Avantir! It had held the Hygerians at bay for long. It had slain many of their best men in the taking. It was a fortress, a symbol of their might. In Avantir, they expected to at least emulate the feat of Ardan's household, keeping back the Asbalnians until time should do its inevitable damage to their cause, until the Hygerians should once more pour across the Mountains, destroying the fragile freedom of Asbaln.

Yet in one wild night of swords, it was swept away.

-The Hygerian War
Randell of Avantir

They came, at last, to the house in the Swamp. They took all the weapons from it, slung in litters improvised from cloaks, and descended into the damp tunnel. Some attempt had been made, with wood shoring, to keep the dampness out of the shaft, but in the lower sections, they waded through water to their knees.

There was room for only one man at a time, a factor which had caused some concern to Rorick, and did to any of the men who gave it a thought. If there were anybody in the storeroom through which the tunnel entered the castle, one powerful warrior could hold the entrance of the tunnel for long enough that the alarm could be raised. Indeed, they might simply fall one by one as they came out into the castle.

Rorick, with the foremost five, rushed straight out into the room as soon as they had opened the door, swords ready for any opposition. The room was empty, save for the stored weapons and other items within it. The Hygerians had left the weapons stored there and had added some of their own to the stock. Rorick called the captains and under-captains of his force around him and knelt on the floor.

In the flickering light of the torches carried by his men, he sketched a plan of that part of the castle important to them in the floor's dust. He looked up at Beran. "We will want groups of ten men stationed here, here, and here, and in this corridor here. Unless we are very unfortunate, they should be enough to hold the way open until we can bring our comrades out from the dungeon. And I will want fifty men to stand in the shadows out here, remaining quiet and unseen unless the rest of us are trapped inside. It will then be necessary for that group to open the gate and send up the signal. With only fifty, it is unlikely that you will be able to hold long enough, but you will have to try."

He cast a smiling look around the room. "But that will not happen. We are in their midst, and they do not know it; even should some warrior or warriors stumble on us, I think we are more likely to carry out our plan before they can organize themselves. Now Beran will assign you to your tasks." He stood and brushed off his hands.

In a series of short concise statements, Beran assigned the men to their tasks, then they set out. Rorick spoke softly:

"Now comes the last of the Guardians' line,

In secret to his ancestral hall;

By hidden ways to the midst of foes,

And by the Sword will stand or fall."

Rorick led them to the dungeons, leaving off the little groups at their appointed places. They met no one. Finally, at the last corner, they heard the sound of Hygerian voices. A careful look showed five men leaning on spears, telling stories. Rorick made some quick signs and led the first ten men around the corner in a rush. The guards had no time to give any alarm.

Most of the men were held in the larger dungeons, a little over two hundred of them. They passed out what arms they had brought, then retraced their steps. Then they had returned to the storeroom. Rorick announced to the new men, "Our task here is not only to set you free, but to open the gates and hold them open for Conel and the war-host. It is time we did that. We will therefore leave you here to arm yourselves, and when you have accomplished that, come out to meet us at the gates.".

OUTSIDE, THEY HAD marked all the sentries nearest the gates, and archers had been assigned to see that they could not interfere. Rorick gave the signal, and they rushed for the gate. As they began to open the huge gates, arrows hissed quickly up at the walls. As might be expected, it was not possible to silence so many men swiftly; shouts of alarm arose, taken up by other sentries around the walls.

The five flaming arrows mounted into the air, and the Warriors took a formation in front of the gate. Looking around, Rorick called "Beran! Assign fifty men to the walls, above the gates."

After that, for a time, all was quiet, save for the occasional hum of a bowstring and shout as another Hygerian a sentry or just a man wandering outside, was seen. However much time might be needed until the prince arrived, Rorick would be grateful for every instant granted them before the Hygerians began to make determined assaults on them.

Before the first Hygerian assaults cue, the last of the Warriors were armed and outside. It was, however, a near enough thing that the last of them were still taking places when the first Hygerians were near enough to throw their javelins. But the arrows of Asbaln were not idle either, and though the skilled archers among them were few, Rorick had seen to it that every man who could be trusted to shoot an arrow elsewhere than into his own foot or into his comrade was armed with a bow.

The first attack was about fifty men, perhaps a detail assigned for emergency policing duty, and in what seemed to be the usual Hygerian manner, they charged without assessing what they might be facing. They failed, of course, but the Warriors took their first casualties. The second attack was better thought out, more men, but the arrows of the Warriors were flying even before they were near enough to make their javelins count. They charged home, though, and only the skill of the Warriors and their fighting ferocity enabled them to hold.

At last the foe drew back, having suffered badly. The Warriors suffered too, but they were now given some respite. The Hygerians, their first thought being that Asbalnians were coning over the walls, were unwittingly encouraged in that delusion by the men over the gate. This allowed some respite for the men in the gateway while the Hygerians untangled the confusion in which they found themselves.

There was still no sign of Conel and the war-host. Rorick stepped forward to be seen and turned to speak to the men. "The Prince ought to have been here by now; whether he is delayed or prevented from coming altogether, I know not, but we must hold here until he comes."

For an answer, he heard a massed shout of "Avantir!" as he returned to his place.

Chapter Fourteen

Rorick was the first grand strategist of his time, and Conel was his best pupil. His encounter-battle with the Hygerians at Dryx ford showed his ability to react instantaneously, to force the battle to follow a shape he forced upon it, and to counter enemy stratagems so promptly it seemed he anticipated them.

Nor was he content with a victory. He knew the position in which Rorick and his men stood. He knew that he could not afford the day's time lost in the battle and the necessary rest and regrouping after, so began an immediate forced march on the next day.

-The Hygerian War
Randell of Avantir

The Hygerians tried cavalry next, charging over the cobbles stones, their horses' shoes throwing up sparks as they came in, determined to ride down the men in the gateway. The Warriors remained steady, bending their bows and loosing with a strange calmness. As the horsemen came closer, some of them cast their javelins at the men facing them. At that time, Rorick shouted a command and a line of spearmen moved forward through the ranks of archers to present a line of glittering spear-points to a seemingly invincible charge.

They did not halt it entirely; it was dim enough that the horses did not see, until the last moment, what they were charging against, and thus many of them impaled themselves. But they destroyed the effectiveness of the charge, for though that front rank of spearmen was broken up and thrown back, the horses in the second rank piled up against those in the first rank, stumbled over the dead and dying men and horses. Into this disorganization stepped the Warriors, shields up, swords ready, and in moments those of the cavalry who could were retreating.

They had a rest for some time as the Hygerian commanders conferred. Rorick inspected his men. “All of you with bows. See to it that every arrow counts. They will come this time determined to destroy us, and we must hold this gate a little longer.”

From above the gate someone called down, “Milord, five flaming arrows over the forest!”

“That will be the Prince. Hold fast, now. Help comes.”

Yet he wondered privately just how far in the forest the war-host might be. He knew the road through there was not one which would allow for great numbers of men to pass swiftly, and it would most certainly be a while before enough men could come through to them.

Then the Hygerians were coming again, perhaps five hundred of them, advancing in grim and purposeful lines across the courtyard. Rorick noted they were a more disciplined and organized lot than most Hygerian infantry they had met so far.

Their arrows did much to equalize the numbers before the foe-men reached them, though the javelins at close range made up for that to some degree. It was in the hand-to-hand fighting the decision was made; iron clashed, swords flickered and thrust, and men fell. Only one incident of that struggle remained with him, when a huge Hygerian swung an axe at him, a blow he caught squarely on his shield and felt it buckle under the impact. For the rest, it was cut, thrust, parry, with no time for noting the man one fought against.

Suddenly the Hygerians were retiring, leaving corpses piled in front of the Asbalnian line. “We cannot stand against another such attack, Milord,” said Beran, at Rorick’s elbow. “If our Prince does not arrive soon, there will be few enough of us here to greet him.”

Rorick’s grim look fell upon him. “There is a resolve upon me, having once more gazed upon my ancestral home, that the gates should not be closed again while I yet live. Speak to the men, lead out those who wish to go, but I will not leave Avantir while it remains in the hands of the Hygerians."

"Too late, Milord, they come again."

And it was true. As well as surging across the courtyard once more, they had parties moving around the wall as well, intent on removing the Asbalnians above the gate. As they moved across the light of one of the torches, Rorick recognized the lean, pinched features contrasting with the plump body of the man who led them, Draxon!

Then behind them was the sound of hooves, and shouts of "Make way! Make way for the Horsemen!"

Through the intervals in the Asbalnian ranks they came, long lances lowered, and infantry, dusty and sweating from a long march, came behind them. Rorick turned to Beran. "Ten men to follow me!"

Then he was headed for the wall.

Chapter Fifteen

Swiftly flashed the traitor's sword,
Swift for the throat, the bright blade sought;
Swifter still moved Avantir's Lord,
As on the castle walls they fought.
Upon the wall did Draxon leap,
And downward did his long blade gleam.
Upward then the Sword did sweep,
And the traitor fell to Ilcaniar's stream.
-from "The Death of Draxon" Conel of Asbaln

Rorick picked a clear path across the courtyard, but some Hygerians blundered into their way and went down in a few slashing moments. At the top of the wall, Draxon was trying to organize his men to throw javelins down into the Asbalnians. Rorick and his men attacked, and for a time all was confusion. With a part of his mind, the guardian sought to work his way toward Draxon, while still fighting with all skill.

Suddenly, the battle was over. The Hygerians were dead or dying, and Draxon stood back a few paces, sword lowered. He wore Hygerian dress and armour, probably for much the same reason that the Asbalnians had cut off the spikes from the captured helmets and shields they used. "Come, traitor, fight!"

Draxon's lips curled. "So speaks Avantir's pampered cub, who never knew want, never worried whether or not the crops would come in. *I* ruled Cair Canlon, where a good year meant only an easing of poverty. Come, then. I fear not death, but if I live, I shall be poor again." He raised his blade and grinned. "Who knows? If any of the reports I hear are true, your Prince may award me Avantir when I have slain you, as a price for my aid. For I *am* of a noble family."

Rage came onto Rorick then, and he stepped forward. A voice spoke in his mind, the voice of Beran on the practice grounds of long-gone years. "Fight with your anger, Lord, and it will slay you surely as though you fell on your sword."

He slowed his advance, calming himself. Draxon, seeing this and guessing the reason, stepped forward to meet him. The traitor baron had misled other men with his bulk, which precluded the speed of movement he showed.

Rorick caught a blow on his shield where the Hygerian's axe had weakened it, and it split in two. Rorick dropped it and attacked again. They traded blows, Rorick at a disadvantage with no shield, until Rorick worked himself into a position where he swung a vicious backhand stroke which ought to have caught Draxon in the right side. The baron managed to partially interpose his shield, so that the blow caught the edge of the shield. There was an audible crack as the handgrips tore away, and Draxon was without a shield.

Rorick had to dodge the next blows because the shield was caught on the Sword, but he worked it loose. Then they both fought with swords alone.

Rorick was never sure how long the rest of the fight took, but it felt as though he and Draxon took turns at holding the advantage, driving each other backward along the wall. Then Draxon, dodging a lunge, leaped up into an embrasure and struck downward at Rorick. The Guardian parried, thrust upward. This time the blow went home, and Draxon fell backward without a sound.

A little later, there was a splash from below. Rorick turned to find Beran nearby. "How many Warriors have we left?"

"We lost a little over fifty dead, possibly another fifty badly wounded. But the Dark ones lost more. The battle is nearly over."

"Aye, this will be a great discouragement for Razak's lords, I am thinking. Have you seen the Prince?"

"Only moments ago he was in the courtyard at the gate, where there is still fighting."

"Well then, shall we stand here all the night while others recover our home for us? Let us go."

Rorick had time to strike only one or two more blows for the restoration of his ancestral home, for organized resistance by the Hygerians was at an end. Some fought on, stubbornly, in corners where they were found, some escaped through the main gate, and through the lesser gates, and a few even surrendered.

Then, with dawn flaming red over the swamp behind them, Rorick found his Prince. The red crest was sheared away from Conel's helmet, and the left cheekpiece was dented by a blow which, miraculously, had barely scratched his cheek. His sword-arm had two long gashes in it, and there was a slash across his right knee. There was no doubt that he had fought for his kingdom.

Beside him stood Donal Two-sword, with only one slight wound, a small cut on his left cheek. He was a more cheerful person now than the grim-faced warrior who had come to them at Orden.

The Prince strode forward to greet Rorick. "Ah, Rorick, that was a battle among battles. We were unavoidably late. We met a force of Hygerians at Dryx ford. They tried to spread out around our flanks, but I divided the Horsemen, bent their own flanks back, and marched the infantry through their centre when they drew men back to the flanks.

"I have noticed that their infantry seem better-trained, more disciplined and ready to fight than ever before. I think we have taught them too much."

"But you came."

"Aye, we came. We dared not march that same day, but in the next days, I forced the march as much as I dared. We were still too far off when the signal went up. I do not quite understand this sudden decision of theirs to march out against us, but it nearly worked. Ah, well, we had accepted a risk, and it turned out well."

"It did. And when we have rested, we must begin planning to move over the Mountains. And that will be difficult, for they will be guarded."

"But let that be for when we have rested. May I ask hospitality of you, Lord of Avantir?"

"The hospitality of my house is always yours, King of Asbaln. I fear you shall find us in some disorder here for a few days, but we shall do what we are able. Indeed, without you, I would not be Lord of Avantir." He turned to Beran. "Beran, can you find for me someone able to act as the part of steward? Someone well able to improvise, I think."

"It shall be done, Milord Guardian."

Chapter Sixteen

Most who are called wise, and many who would disclaim that title, will admit that the High Powers have reasons for all which come to pass, though to Mortal men on earth, the reasons are not always readily apparent.

The Icarian Pass was blocked and forgotten, so thoroughly the Hygerians were never aware of it. It was thus that the men of Asbaln were able to cross the Mountains to take the Hygerians by surprise. And, eventually, Asbaln grew to outshine Hygeria.

Then, when Asbaln had grown old and corrupt, Darkon the Vakon Sea-roving Prince who had become Captain of the Guardian's Warriors, received the Sword from the hands of the dying Guardian, last of his line. And, supported by the Sword, he forged a kingdom from the four baronies east of the Mountains which held for twenty years of his reign, and was passed to his son.

And his son was Rorick of the Iron Hand.

-Avantir, the Kingdom Out of the Ruins
Ammerlyn

Among the many things discussed in the next few days was the task Donal had undertaken. The Old One spoke of the task to Conel and Rorick, and other than Donal, they were the only ones to hear the tale. They agreed he had done more than should be expected of a man fighting for a country, not his. Over his protests, he was assigned command of the castle of Avantir.

In two weeks, the army marched again. The direct route to the pass took them past the haunted forest, and it was here the rumours grew more intense about the task Donal had undertaken. It was commonly agreed he had fought the goblins within the forest of Tarrallalla Banarra, though the details of the battle varied with the man who told the tale.

In the two weeks since the taking of Avantir, skirmishing bands had been making life uncomfortable for the Hygerians on this side of the Mountains, and more and more of them made their way across the Mountains. Some even went through the Pass, and the defenders, being few, let them go rather than fight against desperate men.

And the army of Asbaln, on the road, came upon several little pathetic groups carrying what they could on carts or wagons, and striving to reach the pass. Worse still were the burned out farmsteads where men looked and cursed the Hygerian barbarians until they found that the family who had been massacred there was dark of complexion and had jet-black hair.

For two weeks they attempted the pass, but the pass was so narrow there was no room for manoeuvre, and the Hygerians had a stubborn determination which made the holding of their position a matter of course. They had erected a low barricade of stones, and had stocked innumerable javelins behind the rocky wall, enough to hinder any attackers until they came to close quarters. And no man ever called the individual Hygerian a poor fighter.

For two weeks they attempted all manner of stratagems and failed. Then, in returning from another unsuccessful attack, Rorick heard a young Hillman telling an Asbalnian, “I’d almost as lief try the Icarian pass.”

“Why not tie bundles of your arrows to your arms and flap your way over the mountains? As sensible as going through mythical passes.”

“No myth. With my own eyes I have seen it, though I’d not want the task of clearing this way.”

Rorick stopped them. “This is truth? There is another way through these mountains?”

The Hillman, a handsome young man in a cat-skin tunic and kilt with a long green feather in his hair, answered,

"It is true, Milord Guardian. But that is Lycar's Pass, and may not be used until the hero clears the way."

"Why has this way not been spoken of before?"

"Little use if it had been. By magic, the pass was blocked long ago, and in the old days, many went in, but none came out."

Rorick spoke to Conel on the same subject later on. "What of this Icarian Pass?"

"Ah, yes. In my time in the Hills, I was shown the pass. The entrance is narrow, blocked by a vast mirror, and on the mirror are these words: 'This way is closed to all, until he comes who bears the Power to face the dangers beyond.'"

"How and by whom was the pass blocked?"

"You have heard of Lycar, the Icarian magician?"

"The one who brought forth the legendary dragons?"

"No legends, they. Long ago, after Conel the Wild had united all who speak the Asbalnian tongue, he died more at peace than he lived. His son Ilach, sometimes called the Rash, sought more glory for Asbaln and so sent his hosts into the Hills. The Hillmen resisted him valiantly, and in the end won a truce and a peace.

"But during the time of that war, Lycar determined to block the near-secret Icarian Pass, lest the Asbalnians discover the way and be enabled to send an army secretly into the midst of the Hills. He was not a good man, indeed. Some called him evil, and he drew his spells from places most men would avoid. All one night, he worked in deepest secrecy.

"They say that one of his spells turned on him and drove him mad, and with that same madness, he erected his barrier across the Pass. In the morning, the mirror lay across the pass, and dragons occasionally wandered forth from this mirror, dragons more fierce and hard to kill than those known to inhabit the mountains. It was found men might step through the mirror readily, but none ever returned. After some time, men left the pass alone, left it to slip into legend."

Rorick stood up. "It is in my mind I must try to clear the Pass," he declared.

"And I am thinking you have lost your senses. None has returned from the Pass, and we have need of you here."

"Look closely at the situation, my friend. We might sit here for months and go no further. We might go to the coast and seek out enough ships to ferry our host around the end of the Mountains. If we are able to find the ships and can convince enough ship's masters to undertake the task, they will know we are coming. Will they not certainly be watching and waiting for us to attempt to land?

"And we might march down through the Hills and circle the end of the Mountains. Again, they will surely know we are coming, and will be able to wait for us. And in either of those cases, they may be able to defeat us simply by denying us the supplies we will need. If we can come through the Mountains unknown to them, if we can appear suddenly where they do not expect us, we have that much more advantage.

"And they say that the inscription of the mirror says 'until he comes who bears the Power;' we know the Sword bears a great deal of power. It is in my mind the Sword has the power needed for this task. I shall be going with or without your permission, but I would prefer to have your blessing."

"You are not to be stopped? How could I refuse my blessing on you, who have given to my land her pride, and have given to me most of my Kingdom? But if you do not return, the sun and the stars will turn dark in the sky." True concern was written on the Prince's face.

"It is in my mind that an extremely determined group of men could win this fight here, if they recked not of wounds or death. Even should *I* fail, perhaps I might see that you succeed here.".

THE NEXT DAY, before he left, Rorick assembled the Warriors.

"You know where I go, and that I may not come back. I should be gone no longer than three weeks, and if I have not returned then, you shall know that there is no longer Sword nor Guardian. At that time, you shall no longer be under my orders, and will be free to take whatever service you desire. Yet for those of you who would do a thing in my memory, I could ask no more than this pass should be opened for the Prince.

"Fear not. I shall return while the Sword serves me, and I believe its power will see me safely through. Yet no man is immortal, nor completely invincible, and only a fool does not admit that he, too, may die. So I leave you, and I leave you with my good wishes, and hope to see you again.".

ON HIS SECOND NIGHT of travelling toward Carill Don, he was wakened shortly after he went to sleep. His hand had gone to the hilt of the Sword automatically, and he felt what had wakened him had been a burst of light. There seemed to be a dim shadow over beside the remnant of the fire, a robed man with a staff.

In a quick movement, the figure stamped the butt of the staff down on the ground, and suddenly flames grew from the upper end. In the light, Rorick saw an old grey man, slight of build, slim-featured, and though he leaned on the staff as one wearied with age, something told Rorick this man was more than he seemed. "You go to the Icarian Pass, trusting in the power of the Sword."

"What do you know of that?"

"Great things are moving. The flux of events takes certain courses. And when the Sword is involved, one who knows what he sees can discover much. And you trust in the power of the Sword?"

"Why not? Has the Sword not served me well in several circumstances?"

"Ah, but was the Sword using you, or did it answer your request? Does the Sword simply give you all protection, or does it protect you when you require it?"

Rorick thought for a moment. "It seemed to me when I needed to use the Power of the Sword, I knew how to use it. What is it you are trying to say?"

"I am saying this. You are walking blithely into one of the most complicated traps ever devised by the mind of a madman. No man, I think, could clear the pass unaided by great power. A man with some kind of power might pass through, might even survive, but he must be a man aware at all times. And if, as it appears, you intend to go in feeling the Sword will protect you with no need for you to do anything, why you will probably survive for less time than a man who entered depending on his might and weapon-skill."

Rorick looked the men over, noting the flames on the end of the staff were not burning the Sword in the least. "Do you come to me like this? What concern is it of yours what I do?"

"For yourself, my dear young Guardian, your loss within the pass would sadden me as does the death of any of the many young men who are dying in this war. Yet it is not for that which I come, but that the Sword should not be lost. You do not know what forces are at work in this world, what dread beings will feel free to move when the Sword disappears into that barrier. And when it comes not forth, then will be a time of woe for all men."

"Riddles and mysteries, old man. You look like no Hygerian, nor yet like one who would hinder us in our war, yet you speak of some dread danger which will befall us if take the Sword into the Pass. Surely you know strange tales will not deter me."

Within those eyes, at the same time seeming both summer-rain grey and deep-sea blue, a flash of humour appeared. "My young Lord, will it in any way ease your mind to know that those same strange forces and beings I spoke of will also move if it should come to pass that the Hygerians are victorious? I know you have looked to your strategy, have made your evaluations, and have decided you must try the Pass. I simply wish you will bring the Sword forth again. For this reason, you must be aware that it is yourself who decides to use the power of the Sword, and the Sword will respond only to your desire. Do not expect it to leap into your hand when it is needed."

Rorick was silent for a moment, then he asked, "Can you tell me what I shall meet behind the barrier?"

"Can I tell you whether fall will be early or late this year, whether the snows of this winter will be light, or whether men must remain in their houses for weeks on end? You go into a trap built by a madman, where what is at one moment is not at the next. It is for you to watch what arises, see when matters require the power of Sword, and where it is your weapon skill which is to be tested. To this degree, may I warn you, that you beware always for what may not be what it seems."

"So you have come to tell me not to depend on the Sword."

"I have come to tell you not to depend on the Sword to do your fighting for you. Use the Sword, use your mind, but do not count yourself safe because you bear the ultimate talisman against powers of magic. We have been speaking too long, with too little understanding. Now I have said what I would say, and may it go well with you."

"May I ask your name?"

"My name? I am Ammerlyn, and you have no doubt heard of me. Farewell, Lord of Avantir" The flame at the end of the staff flared into sudden brightness, and when Rorick could see again, the old man was gone. He sat still for some time, wondering at what he had seen and heard. Ammerlyn, the Wandering Wizard, the figure of a thousand legends! Yet surprisingly, sleep came easily to him..

WHEN HE AT LAST reached Carill Don, he stayed there but one night. Helana listened to him and was sad, but said nothing against his plan, though the Chief and one or two others tried to argue with him. When the two were at last alone, he smiled at her. “Will you not also try to dissuade me from this mad project?”

She shook her head. “No, for it is in my heart that you will not be stopped. May the High Ones go with you.”

Chapter Seventeen

High on the rocks where the eagles scream,
The Guardian enters the madman's dream.
Armed with Power in his right hand,
Goes he into the magic land.
Behind he leaves the brown-tressed maid,
Helana the Hill-daughter, unafraid.
Ahead, do danger and death await;
And what will be the Guardian's fate?
-from 'The Clearing of the Pass,'
Artir One-eye of the Midland Plain.

The next morning, they went to the Pass. While they were yet some distance away, they rested on a hillock while Helana pointed out certain of the peaks and named them.

She pointed first to one which sloped gently from its bottoms, then more steeply, then leaped suddenly into a sheer pinnacle of snow-blanketed rock. "There is the one we call *Kinsetchgrityotch*, The White Needle of Rock, and there beside it," she pointed to one with a large, many-rayed patch of snow on a purple face, "that is *Hnigrikskroitotch*, The Star in the Rock Above the Darth. Down between them it runs, *Harralgriksymba*. the Evil Way Through the Rocks."

They continued on their way, and soon stood before the great mirror, which spanned a significant gap between two sheer cliffs. Hear its base, directly at the point where the old path disappeared beneath the mirror, was an inscription. At first glance, the letters were blurred and illegible; on closer inspection, however, they seemed to leap into brilliant life, reading in this way:

"This way is closed to all,

Until he comes who bears the Power

To face the dangers beyond."

Rorick looked down at Helana, who was trying to smile through her fear. He leaned down to kiss her, saying, "It would be useless to tell you not to worry, but I will say that you give me an added reason to wish to return."

Then, drawing the Sword, he lifted his shield and stepped through the mirror. He felt the hilt of the Sword tingle, then he was inside. He stood looking over a wide and desolate Plain, which extended miles in all directions. Before him stood a low stone, stone marker, with words written upon it. When he looked at them, he saw this: 'You who have dared to pass through the barrier, prepare to meet the first peril.'

Then a circle of flame appeared before him, and through that circle came a man, mounted on a great boar, wearing a breastplate of bronze and a helmet of copper, bearing in his hands three javelins. He looked at the Guardian and cried, "Choose how you shall fight! Either fight myself without your shield, my steed without your sword, or the both of us with sword and shield!"

Rorick looked at the two of them, considered the difficulty of fighting the boar bare-handed, or warding off javelins without a shield, and said, "I shall fight the two of you, With sword and shield."

With no further word, the man kicked at the boar's flanks and charged, casting a javelin as he came. Rorick's shield came up far enough to ward the boar off, but not so far that it blocked his sight. With a leap, he dodged the boar's slashing tusk, swinging a backhand stroke as he did so.

It was not a particularly solid blow and should rightly have only angered the animal. But the boar stumbled forward onto its knees, flinging its rider free, and suddenly flared into blue flames.

But the rider was up on his feet and whirling like a dancer. Rorick moved in quickly, shield up. The man hurled his second javelin, which the Guardian warded off, and leaped back and sideward, keeping back from the Sword. Now they began a careful dance, the boar-rider seeking to keep back from the Sword, and find an opening sure enough for his javelin, Rorick seeking to close with him.

The battle ended at last, when the man found himself at an angle and cast the javelin with all his strength, a cast which left him bent at an awkward angle. Rorick, bending and twisting his own body, avoided the worst of the blow, though it cut through his armour and gashed his side above the hip. But he was back on balance quickly enough and leaped forward with the Sword outthrust.

His opponent, who had been more off-balance, was just slow enough in moving that the tip of the Sword touched his throat. It ought to have been a wound of the same severity as a man might cause to himself in shaving, but there was a blaze of blue flames, and the helmet and breastplate lay on the ground, with only a touch of discolouration.

After recovering from his astonishment, Rorick set about bandaging his wound to the best of his ability. Because of its location, the wound was difficult to deal with, but he ended by tucking a wad of cloth inside, and arranging his war-shirt to hold the make-shift bandage fast.

This done, he looked around. The desolate waste was still empty, but a path now led from the stone marker off toward the horizon. "And if that was there when first arrived, best I should use my helmet as a beggar-bowl, and sit at the gates for blind," muttered Rorick.

He thought about the battle he had just fought, and he knew that the power of the Sword had absorbed whatever magic which had produced the boar and its rider, and he wondered what might be the next test? He took a step along the path..

IT HAD BEEN a strange sensation, and he now stood on a different road, a road which seemed to be a lone continuous ribbon of stone. The sun in the sky above was not yellow, but violet, and his eyes required some time to become familiar with the strange colouration. Off to his left rear was a line of towers, towers built of metal bars, stretching out as far as he could see, and crossing the road at an angle before him to reach again to the horizon. There seemed no reason to hesitate here. He stepped forward..

HE STOOD IN A CLEARING in a darkened wood, a low stone marker before him. On the marker he could read the words, which glowed a little in the dimness: "You have passed the first of the tests. Now you must spend the night in this forest, a test of your fears. He who fears nothing may survive."

Rorick considered this. He smiled grimly, and said, "Yet it does not say that he will not survive who knows fear."

He was immediately aware of the sound of feet moving in the surrounding woods, paralleling his path, following him, stalking ahead of him. When he stopped, the sounds stopped, save for a steady approach of feet behind him. He hastened on. The movements around him continued. Suddenly, he broke into a run. All around him, the beings, whatever they were, kept pace with him.

The darkness was near complete now, and he darted full-tilt into a low tree-branch. His helmet saved him from more than a stunning blow and a fall, but he regained some sense with it. Rorick could not possibly defend himself properly here on the trail, should they decide to attack him, since they could approach within feet of him without being seen. He went back down the trail to the clearing with the marker. He would have to fight his way past the one behind him, but it would give him a better chance if he were successful.

The things in the surrounding bush kept pace with him, and one had taken to the trail in his rear, but he neither saw nor heard the one he had expected to have to fight. He finally stumbled into the clearing again, and stood by the stone marker, turning slowly to look in all directions, waiting for the first attack.

The attack did not come immediately. He saw no sign of the stalkers, but he heard them gathering ail around, heard them moving and shifting in the brash. Then, with still no attack, he made a fire; it might serve to keep them back at least a little. Carefully, never letting the Sword out of his hand, he gathered dry wood together. Then he had enough. He made some kindling and set up the wood for the fire. He squatted down and said his fire-spell.

At first, nothing came of it; on the second attempt, a burst of flame consumed the wood almost immediately, and only the fact that he flung himself backward saved him from a nasty burn. He got to his feet, looking around; still none of the watchers were in sight. "So magic works strangely here," he said.

He found a few coals remaining from the wood he had set for the fire, and on this, he built a new one. Still nothing came out of the brash, though the sounds continued. Behind him was always noise as of something preparing to attack, and just when he thought they had burst into the clearing, he turned. There was nothing, and the noise subsided. Again and again this happened, and each time there was no attack.

His nerves were tense, every movement which seemed nearer than the rest brought him nearly leaping around. Suddenly, directly in front of him, a beast came out of the brush. It might have been a lion designed by a madman, for the shape and the man were there, but the beast was a grey dust-colour, and had three pairs of legs, each ending in clawed feet. It charged at him, emitting a noise midway between a growl and a roar, and sprang the last ten feet.

What Rorick did then was more the result of much practice than of considered thought. The shield came up to ward off the front claws and the mouthful of gleaming teeth, and the Sword thrust out for the grey beast's chest. The force on the shield sent him staggering, and the Sword was wrenched from his hand. He kept his feet and saw the strange blue flames begin to consume the first beast, and saw others slinking forward out of the brush.

His only weapon now was his dagger, for the Sword was in the flaming chest of the first monster. He saw death coming, for the Sword had been barely sufficient for the first strike. Fear overwhelmed him, and the grey pack closed in. Something in his mind whispered:

"Die fighting, you fool!"

He drew his dagger, squared his shoulders, and said:

"Grey pack, fierce pack, many fangs you bear,

But one tooth alone have I, which to rend and tear.

Only death you bring to me, fear I set aside;

Who is first to come to the first to risk his hide?"

There was hesitation in the circle of monsters. Rorick laughed. "No, it was not my best poem, but then are you the judges? Come, I have but one foot of steel here, enough for all of you, too much, perhaps, for one or two"

A chorus of howls rose, howls with a note of frustration. Slowly, all together, they backed off into the brush again. For a time there was the sound of the heavy bodies retreating into the depths of the brush, then silence, save for the crackling of the two fires, his own, and the burning carcass.

The body burned for a long time, and it was some time even after that before he was able to recover the Sword. Yet in all that time, he heard nothing of the beasts. When the Sword was finally cool enough to be touched with his bare hand, he sheathed the sword and sat leaning against the stone marker. A little later, he slept.

In the morning, after a few moments spent stamping some of the stiffness out of his limbs, he set out along the road again. At his first step past the marker, he wondered what was in store for him.

HE WAS ON the desolate plain again beneath the purple sun. Off to the right was a collection of what seemed to have once been buildings of magnificent stature, perhaps an entire city. But all seemed to have been smitten in some dreadful way, broken, cloven, half shattered. He wondered, as he stepped along the road, what might have wrought such devastation?

HE STOOD BEFORE an immense wall, featureless save for the holes which were mounted in a line before him. Carven into the black rock, at the level of his eyes, were these words:

"Choose now whether you shall take with you the shield proof against all, or attempt the coming tests without it."

He thought for a moment. Knowing what he had seen already, a shield proof against all ought to be invaluable for the rest of the tests. Yet he doubted the shield was simply there for the taking; the method of claiming the shield would be a test in itself. He climbed the wall, watching warily for any trap, for my sign of some foe waiting above. Unmolested, he came to the top of the wall.

The wall stretched out as far as the eye could see, without break or waver, and was a good ten yards wide. In the centre, just ahead of him, a shield was set into the surface of the wall. Rorick approached it and saw that the shield was essentially the same as his, though the upraised Sword in the centre of it was brighter and newer than on his. He bent to reach for the shield, but his fingers could not touch it. He straightened and saw a shimmer in the air before him.

The shimmer thickened, darkened, and before he could guess at what it might be, solidified into a man, eight feet tall, well-muscled, wearing what appeared to be a cuirass of leather and a bronze helmet. He bore a rectangular shield on his left arm, and on his right, he held an axe with a short, stout handle. When he spoke, his voice had a strange quality, as though it came from far away.

"I am here to guard the shield. Here in my hand I bear the axe proof against all. Now you have chosen, and now you may go down alive with the shield, or dead without."

The axe swung up and down. Rorick raised the Sword and brought his shield into position. The axe rent his shield as though it was made of cloth, and he barely managed to save his left arm, missing his return-stroke in doing so. Three more such blows left his shield a useless ragged lump of metal and wood. He dropped his shield, avoided a blow of the axe, and swung the Sword. The other caught it on his shield, and the shield buckled.

Then the dread axe was descending, and Rorick parried with the Sword; Rorick felt the two weapons' edges jarring together, and was blinded by a brilliant flash. He was lying on his back, looking up at the purple sky, with no idea of how he had come there. He sat up, and his right arm felt dead. The Sword lay in front of him, a small blackened patch on its blade.

The axe, a lump of fused and blackened metal, lay a little further on, and just beyond it was the burned body of the shield's guardian, slain by the force unleashed at the meeting of the two weapons of Power. Rorick stood. He took up the Sword in his left hand and looked around. He approached the shield, which now seemed to sit loosely on the surface of the wall.

After a moment, there being no sign of any further interference, he clumsily sheathed the Sword, and picked up the shield. Some feeling was slowly returning to his arm now, and he could move it enough to fix the shield on his left arm.

RORICK WAS ON THE ROAD through the desolate plain, his right hand still on the shield. He stood still, knowing that each time before, his first step on that road had taken him to the next test, and he did not wish to attempt the next test with his right arm still half dead. Rorick viewed his surroundings.

On a hill, to his left front, was the remains of a single building, its walls standing ragged against the violet sky. The ground around the building was pitted, and in some places melted to a glassy sheen. Strange machines lay all around the building, most of them obviously broken and twisted. Wondering again what could have wrought such devastation, he stepped forward.

HE WAS FACING AN enormous cliff, extending for miles in either direction. Just in front of him there was a large fissure in the cliff, and within the fissure was a marker, bearing these words:

"Hurry, O hero, for your destination lies through here."

He would have stepped in, but caution held him back. Further in, on the left-hand side, was a deep cup-like depression, with grooves leading down from it as though water running out of it had worn channels in the rock.

Shrugging, he stepped forward, extending the Sword before him into the fissure. He hesitated a moment, and was just about to move further in when a stream of liquid spurted from a hole in the left-hand side, striking the cup-depression on the right-hand side. He watched as it hissed and crackled, and he could see it dissolving before his eyes.

His imagination told him what would have happened had that liquid touched him, and he now knew why he had taken the shield proof against all. Carefully positioning the shield, he stepped into the fissure. The liquid streamed out, striking the shield, and ran down to drip onto the rock floor of the fissure, crackling and hissing as it did so.

As he reached the other end of the fissure, he breathed a deep sigh of relief. “I wonder how many came here and stepped straight in without hesitation? Even this shield would have failed to protect me had I been carrying it less carefully. Powers Above, what strange place have I fallen into?” He sighed again. “Well, it seems to me that the nature of this place is such that I shall either fight my way through to the end or die. So, I must be upon my way, for if I am to die, it will be as near to the goal as I can possibly manage.”

He stepped forward on the path leading out from the fissure.

BEFORE HIM, THE LONG flat road led off to the beginning of some rolling hills, disappearing behind a gentle curve. The road, which was made of a single long piece of rock, was cracked and shattered a little further on, great holes gouged in it, chunks of the road lying around, slabs of it lifted and left lying askew. A train of wagons had been travelling and had been destroyed by the same power. Rorick could only shudder. He took the next step.

BEFORE HIM LAY a cave in a grassy hillside. A tall stone stood alone midway between the Guardian and the cave. He approached the tall stone with caution. Upon the stone hung a brass horn, much the size and shape of an oxhorn, and there was a small plaque below it. Upon the plaque he read these words: “With this horn you may summon a dragon from yonder cave; this dragon you must slay, for his longest fangs are keys which you will need, should you survive to the end.”

Rorick extended his hand, and just before he touched the horn, he stopped. “It does not say we must call the drake forth and stand like fools while it overruns me. Let me think.”

He looked around. There was little of any use in the immediate neighbourhood, save some rather twisted branches. He walked up to the cave. There was no sign of the dragon immediately, but he could not see the entire rear of the cave, for the cave was deep. He frowned, then went back outside. The slope around the cave's mouth was gentle, and he would have no trouble climbing it. But he needed more than that.

He went to a clump of brush, and cut one of the straightest and stoutest poles, about seven feet in length. He had just taken out a length of leather cord from his pack when he looked back at the cave, frowned, and shook his head. "Not enough. It will require a trifle more subtlety."

He went back to the clump, and cut four more, equal length with the first, then went to another clump and cut some more. At last, with twelve of them ready, he took six down into the mouth of the cave and, by digging into the ground and by piling up stones, set them across the mouth of the cave with the ends, cut to sharp points, directed inward and up at an angle.

He moved out to the point where it was not quite possible to turn aside from the path out of the cave. Here he planted the other poles in a similar manner, save that in the centre. He tied his dagger securely to one of them, covering it over with a strip of bark. He surveyed his work, nodded, and went to take down the horn.

Standing just behind the second row of stakes, he set the horn to his mouth and blew. Rorick blew first a long blast, then an improvised call which sounded like pure mockery. He waited, and a moment later heard the noise of dragon-hide scraping on rock as the drake approached. He backed off a little and saw the dragon come up to the first row of stakes.

With a roar, the dragon pushed against the stakes, snapping them off easily with no harm to his hide. He came forward in a rush, careless of the second row, charging full upon Rorick. Wood splintered, the drake flung back his head and gave a hissing scream of pain. Now Rorick moved; running up the slope, just beside the monster, he drew the Sword.

For all the pain of his wound, the dragon was still dangerous; he turned and belched out a gout of flame which

Rorick, who had expected something of the sort, caught mostly on his shield. The Guardian leaped, landing astride the long and scaly neck just behind the head, which was about half as long as his own body.

He locked his legs around the neck and hewed with the Sword; the blow did little more than break a scale or two. He cut again, with little better success, then flung aside his shield and took the Sword in both hands. At this point, the dragon's writhing and bucking became so frenzied that he had to hold himself on with his arms and his legs, or be cast off like a leaf.

For a time, it was all he could do to keep his place. Then, in an instant where the dragon paused infinitesimally, Rorick took the Sword in both hands and struck. He managed two blows before the drake heaved and writhed, sending him flying. The landing jarred him, and though he sought to move quickly to rise and prepare to fight, his limbs would not obey him. But the dragon did not attack; he continued to writhe, scream, and paw at his chest. Suddenly, the drake fell; a moment later he was up again, still screaming, still pawing his chest.

Rorick held back. It was clear that his trap with the dagger was having its effect, and therefore it was no longer necessary to risk all by closing with the beast. The wound on its neck was also making itself felt, and the dragon did not seem interested in avenging itself on the man who had caused its pain.

It took a long while before the dragon was dead, and it took Rorick a little longer to remove the two longest teeth as the instructions on the plaque demanded. At last, with all things ready, he stepped out on the path.

ON THE ROAD BEFORE HIM was a long line of wagons and other conveyances, most destroyed, with whitened skeletons lying amongst them. There were bundles of implements which had survived the destruction and the time which had elapsed, and these were people fleeing from the Power which was unleashed. Rorick took his next step.

A LARGE GREY STONE CASTLE stood in the violet light of the sun. It seemed to be hewn from a single block of stone, for there was no join to be seen in its face. The huge double gate was locked with a padlock the size of his head, and above it was a brazen plate, which he could read when he approached:

"Bold hero, prudent hero. Here is the last of the tests. In the central tower is the Power which blocks the pass, but the dead guard the castle. Use your keys, enter, and prepare to fight."

The padlock had two round holes in it, one above the other. Rorick put one of the dragon's teeth into one of the holes, heard a click, inserted the other, and when it clicked, opened the lock and pushed the gate.

He drew the Sword and stepped in. All around the courtyard stood or sat several skeletons, armed with shield and sword, spear, or axe. As he stepped inside, they became aware of him; heads turned toward him, and those sitting rose, while those standing drew weapons and moved toward him.

Warily, he watched them. Suddenly, the nearest one leaped at him, sword swinging. He caught the blow on his shield, and his return stroke went through the skeleton's guard to bite into its bleached ribs. He felt the tingling sensation in his hand again, and the skeleton fell to the courtyard in a heap of disconnected bones.

Rorick realized then that the Sword could counter the magic which animated the skeletons. Rorick knew he need only touch any of them to render them finally dead. He set himself to fighting toward a wall where his back could be protected. He succeeded in this endeavour but was not totally unscathed after he had achieved it. The foe attacked with a silent ferocity and possessed a weapon-skill only slightly hindered by a hint of slowness.

Then, with ten of their number finally downed, the rest fell back into a small watchful semicircle. Rorick, with several light wounds, leaned on The Sword and huffed. Then, still leaning negligently on it, he sang a small mocking song:

"Swiftly swords under violet sun,

Come to me, dead ones, the battle's not done;

Which bony foe will next be stilled?

For Arvandal's sons are not easily killed.

Come, now, come, I've not the whole day;

Let there be an ending to this play.

Such a little exercise can do no harm,

Though perhaps the sun is a little too warm?"

As though in answer, the castle's grim guardians moved once more to the attack. Rorick had been considering all things, however, and now changed his own methods. Penned in here against the wall, he would eventually be worn down and slain. He therefore leaped to meet the first of them, crashing into him with his weight behind his shield, bowling that one over into the one behind him, and making a path through them. One or two more blows gave him an empty space through which to go, and he ran for the tower.

He had no expectation of outrunning them all, merely getting a good enough head start to deal with less of them at once. He whirled suddenly; the Sword swinging in a huge backhand which beat the skeleton's shield back far enough that the edge of the Sword struck the breastbone, which was enough to drop that opponent.

Two others were coming in at once. He thrust the Sword at one, kicked out hard at the other. Whatever power directed them was making them wary of the Sword, for while his kick sent the one stumbling backward, the other flung himself aside from the flickering blade. Then Rorick leaped backward, turned, and ran again for the tower.

Arriving at the door, he raised the Sword and brought it down in a blow that contained all the strength he could muster. The door cracked. He drew back, but the nearest of his foes was almost upon him. He turned to fight. They were strung out again, and he fought with all the skill and every trick he possessed. Twice he leaped away from blows to fall against the door, which cracked under his weight. Then, as he staggered backward against the door under the weight of one of his attackers charging heedlessly upon him, it broke.

He barely regained his balance, and a quick blow dispatched the skeleton who had fallen inside with him and was now trying to rise. He stepped to the door fast enough to prevent the next one from coming in, and at the threshold, he made his stand.

They could come through only one at a time, and he met each as they stepped through. It was difficult, and as the fight went on, he lost the advantage in quickness which he had had at the beginning. His limbs felt like lead, and the piled bones hindered his feet, though he kicked as many of them aside as he could. Three times he was forced to step back far enough from the doorway that the skeleton against which he presently fought could enter and let in the one or two behind, but each time in sheer desperation he drew up the energy to defeat them and hold the door again. On the third time, when he stepped to the door, he found no more opposition.

He leaned against the door-jamb, breathing heavily. “Powers Above, I am in little better case than they.” His chain-mail was rags of metal, his leg was gashed twice, badly, his right arm cut twice, though not quite so badly, his helmet dented, the crest sheared off, and the sight of his right eye was obscured by blood from a cut above it. He had innumerable other lesser lacerations, and his head swam.

He turned and fell on the steps. Rising, he staggered upward, upward upon the circling stair. Faint, sickening, with only the thought of lives thrown away at the Guardian’s Pass keeping him upright, he made his way to the top of the tower. Another wooden door stood before him, and when he pushed, the door opened and he found a room about ten feet square.

Across the room was a window, looking out on the path along which he had approached. In the centre was a waist-high block of grey stone, with a large crystal sphere atop it. Within the crystal was a small bright violet spark which seemed to becoming brighter and brighter.

Suddenly the sphere became blue, then an angry red. Its colour changed more swiftly now, and it became a searing white, then expanded to fill the inside of the sphere. Shaking off the weariness that gripped him, Rorick raised the Sword. As he approached, the light became so fierce that he hid his face behind the shield.

As he brought the Sword down, there was a bright blue flash, and he was flung against the wall. Then he felt the building shake, and as he turned toward the door, the building fell.

SUDDENLY, HE WAS standing upon the gap between the mountains, on green grass, with a proper yellow sun above. There was an encampment of Icarians before him, and he heard the shouts of alarm and surprise just before he collapsed.

Chapter Eighteen

Rorick and Conel were not, of course, the only men in Asbaln to rise against the Hygerians, nor even the only ones to have a measure of success. Phedron Doubleaxe, to whom was later given the Sevenhills Barony, had developed on his own ideas similar to those used by Conel and Rorick. The news which came over the Mountains to him, encouraged him, and drew more men to join his cause. He was not connected to the old nobility of the land, though there were some rumours about which the truth could not be ascertained. He was, however, not only one of the best among those fighting for the freedom of Asbaln, but was among the best of the new barons.

-The Hygerian War
Randell of Avantir

He awoke briefly the next morning, back at the village. Helana was there. "Quiet, Rorick, rest. You need much sleep."

"They must be told at the pass."

"Do you think we are fools? A messenger left for the Prince as soon as we brought you to the village. Now rest."

Somehow, though, he thought to argue; the words did not come. He drifted into dreams.

IT WAS LATE AFTERNOON, he guessed from the shadows on the wall.

Helana sat in a chair beside him. "The clearing of the pass did not leave you unscathed, my warrior."

"No, but I did return, queen of my heart."

"And for that, I am grateful. It has been a long week that I waited for you."

"A week! Two days, by my counting."

"Yesterday was the seventh day from the time you stepped into the mirror."

Rorick lay still for a moment or two. "That was a strange place indeed. But if it was indeed a week, I must go to the pass."

"You must go nowhere at all for some days. You have several bad wounds, a score of minor cuts, some terrible burns and an assortment of bruises. And there is no reason for you to go to the pass, as the war-host will be coming back here. Now drink this; it will help you sleep."

So firm was her demeanour that Rorick drank the medicine before he could decide that he didn't want to. He lay back and closed his eyes for a moment before telling Helana what he thought of tyrannical women. It was dark when he opened them again.

IN HIS STARTLEMENT, he sat up quickly. He fell back as quickly with a thunderous aching in his head, and he vaguely remembered a blow which had glanced ringingly from the side of his helmet. It died down in a few moments, and he opened his eyes to see Helana leaning over him. A little more cautiously, he sat up.

"Well, it seems that I have slept the day away."

"This day, and yesterday as well. I have never seen a man so tired. You look better now, though perhaps a little hungry."

And Rorick realized then just how hungry he was. She smiled and went out, returning very shortly with a jug of ale and some bread and meat.

"Some of the healers say that a man in your case should not eat too much, but I have a different opinion. I think you will know for yourself when you have had enough."

She spread out the food before him, and as he ate, she asked, "Would you tell me something of what you found beyond the mirror?"

So Rorick recounted, briefly, what had happened behind the mirror. So brief was his story that Helana felt it necessary to interrupt several times with questions in order to find out just what had gone on. When it was done, they sat silently for a little time. Helana spoke at last.

"It is time for you to rest again. Would you care for some music to help you relax?"

"I would indeed. What songs do you know?"

"As you are aware, we of the Hills share a part of the heritage of the folk of Asbaln. Among our people as well as your people, there are the songs of the Old Island, of the Ancient Days."

"Indeed? Do you know the song of Taura Lella Morna?"

"Most certainly." She took up a small harp and stroked it, then began to sing:

"O Taura Lella Morna, nevermore, nevermore!
O Taura Lella Morna, nevermore!
Great towers, white towers, standing proud and tall;
King and Queen and lady fair in white stone hall.
The towers fell in ruins as we sadly sailed away,
From Taura Lella Morna, at the breaking of the day.
O Taura Lella Morna, nevermore, nevermore!
O Taura Lella Morna, nevermore!
Ah, Taura Lella Morna, with the towers white as snow!
Ah, Taura Lella Morna, with the fields green below!
There is sorrow in our hearts, for we nevermore will stay,
In Taura Lella Morna, at the breaking of the day.
O Taura Lella nevermore, nevermore!
O Taura Lella Morna, nevermore!
O Taura Lella Morna, by the sunset, painted gold!
O Taura Lella Morna, fair city built of old!
Now our hearts are sadly breaking, for we nevermore shall sight,
Fair Taura Lella Morna, shining tall in the twilight.
o Taura Lella Morna, nevermore, nevermore!
o Taura Lella Morna, nevermore!
Fair city, white city, that sheltered all our lives;
Great city, doomed city, sorrow cuts like knives!

Though we live till world's end, no city shines so bright,
As Taura Lella Morna, proud and gold in the twilight.
O Taura Lella Morna, nevermore, nevermore!
O Taura Lella Morna, nevermore!
Ships shall bear us safely far across this wild, wide sea;
We shall come to land at last, who cares where that may be?
For where we go, we shall ever bear with us the sight,
Of Taura Lella Morna, dying, burning, in the night.
o Taura Lella Morna, nevermore, nevermore!
o Taura Lella Morna, nevermore!"

When the last notes had died away, Rorick sat silently staring into the last flickering remnants of the fire.

"A beautiful song that," said Helana, "but a song of great sadness as well. And it is time for you to be sleeping again, my hero."

Rorick smiled. "It is a song of beauty indeed, but no less beautiful is she who sings it."

"And my hero, even hacked half to pieces, has a tongue to charm the birds in the sky. Now do you go to sleep and become well."

TWO WEEKS FROM the clearing of the pass, the war-host was once more in the Hills. Two hundred men had remained behind at the pass, to prevent the Hygerians from rushing through when they discovered the absence of the war-host. As Beran put it later, the two forces sat and snarled at each other across their barricades, but did little else.

Conel came to Rorick, his eyes shining, his feet near dancing with his news. "Great news has come, O my brother of the Sword! Three days before we left the pass, a man came over the Mountains to us, and was brought in to me. He told us he had taken a trail across the Mountains to bring us news, and when he saw my face he shook his head and said, 'Na, Milord, 'e was but a track o' th' beasts. A man, ten men, might ga' through, but th' whole host would still be marching when the snows fell.'" Conel smiled at the memory, and Rorick at the mimicry of the accent.

"But his news. There is a sheepherding man named Phedron, in the foothills of the North, who owns his own freehold, crew tired of the continual grasping of the Dark ones, who would take the best of his flocks with no return. He therefore raised his own force and fought. Shortly after we had taken Virdan, he had his own force of mounted archers. At this time, he has a force of three hundred cavalry and seven hundred infantry, with more joining him all the time. He has cleared the Hygerians from all the land of the Sevenhills and made the land north of the Relyn river a disputed territory. Crossing the Mountains will increase our host more than we had thought."

"Good news indeed. When do we march?"

"When you are able. But for now, I will want to hear the tale of your doings in the pass. It is in my mind that it would make for good listening."

Chapter Nineteen

To the King, from the Sevenhills men, this gift:
The steeds of Sevenhills, strong and swift;
Safe from the foe our herds remain,
And their loss is King Conel's gain.
High in the hills, the grass is green,
The fairest land that was ever seen;
Asbaln's men are free there still,
For we are the people of the hill

.

-from 'The Song of the Hills'
Phedron Doubleaxe of the Seven Hills

For all the years of its being blocked, the Icarian pass showed little sign of the passage of years, save only that the trail itself was overgrown in brush and shrubbery. Some of the men, particularly among the Icarians, were not happy about entering the pass of ill omen, whether or not the great mirror was gone from its face. However, with the King and the Guardian leading them, none felt able to hold back.

As they came through the pass to the hills beyond, Conel turned to Rorick. He smiled. "The fellow told me, 'I can't say where 'e'll be, but if ye ga northward, and ga forwardly, 'e'll surely come to ye.' I only hope he made it back across his 'track o' th' beasts' to tell Phedron that we are coming through the Icarian pass."

"How had he intended to bring a thousand or more men down from the Sevenhills country to the Guardian's Pass unseen?"

Conel shrugged. "I could not say, but from the messenger's attitude, I believe he had at least convinced his men that it was not a matter of conjecture, and they *would* be there. I am anxious to meet this Phedron."

The march northward continued, with no sign of the Hygerians being reported. Half a day's march from the mouth of the pass, the Chief of the scouts reported in. He was a little wizened man wearing a leather cap and a jacket and kilt of indeterminate origin, some kind of fur. He carried a light but strong bow decorated with what looked like Elder runes, and at his hip was what was either a long dagger, or a short sword. His speech was, surprisingly, somewhat cultured, though he slipped into dialect on occasion.

"Milord King, we've no sure and certain proof, but it appears we're under observation by someone's scouts. They are not Hygerians, that we can certainly say, but then there's been those working for the Hygerians that have more black heart than black hair. They can evade us because this isn't our own territory, but can guarantee that they'll not ambush us."

Another little man on a pony, looking much as though he were built on the pattern of the Chief of the scouts, came dashing down out of the brush ahead of them, swinging his bow in a wide circle, the agreed-on signal for immediate danger. Conel shouted a quick order, and the war-host shifted itself into line, while the Horsemen formed a quick line, moving forward to screen them until they were prepared. Conel and Rorick moved along with the Horsemen, and out of the clump of woods behind the scout came a small band of horsemen.

They streamed across the slope at a gallop, riding like the Hellriders who hunted Dyn Fawr, the Elder Hero, when he escaped from the Underworld by a trick. From their dress, they were Asbalnians, though much of it was equipment obviously taken from the Hygerians. Most of them carried bows, and as they came nearer, it was apparent that their leader was a large and powerfully built man, bearing a double-bladed axe and wearing a helmet with a pair of white eagle's wings attached.

None of them took weapons in heads, but they dashed straight up to the Prince and pulled up their horses with a shout. The leader, leaning forward on his saddle, grinned and said, "So these are the cubs who have driven the Black Folk from the other side of the Mountains? Welcome, welcome, both of you. I am Phedron, known as Phedron Doubleaxe, and these with me are a few of my men. We fought a battle with the Hygerians yesterday and left a greater part of a thousand of them dead at the crossing of the Relyn.

"I have eight hundred trained men left, but more than enough in training to make up the losses. Only about two thousand Hygerians remain between here and the city of Hardinian. We expect them to send another army after us shortly, but by then we will have another army waiting for them."

"Phedron Doubleaxe, there is joy in my heart to see you. We have some thoughts for the campaign between here and Hardinian. Tonight, with your help, we shall make more final plans."

THE LEADERS OF the war-host sat that night around a large table, Conel at the centre with Rorick and Phedron on each side of him. Besides these were Cyrcom, Trent, and Fergus, Phedron's cavalry leaders, along with Byrt, Hwardh, Furthach, and Lughan, who headed his infantry. The commanders of the Prince's infantry were there also, Artir, Lagan, Verex, and Staranth, with Garth and Cirl, his cavalry captains.

Conel was speaking. "The main road runs from just outside here, where we sit down to Hardinian. Then they hear word that we are here. We will be most certainly expected to come down here. But to the east of that road," he pointed with his dagger at the map, "there is a trail which leads to Hardinian, though only a small one. If a part of the war-host goes down the main road, they will draw the Hygerians to meet them somewhere along the way. Yet if at the same time we send most of the host down the trail here, they ought to come on Hardinian by surprise. If we move quickly, we can take the city before they can organize a proper defence, and having the city will probably draw men away from the force on the main road. Those on the main road will then come to join us, and we may catch their forces between us."

His eagle eyes searched the faces of all the room. Phedron stood. "A question, Milord. What of patrols on this road? Cruel he may be, conqueror and tyrant he most certainly is, but Razak is not a fool. And I've no doubt that he knows the land near as well as most in your host, milord, since, begging your pardon, you are mostly Eastern men, and few of you have actually ridden that trail through the hills."

"Boldly and well spoken, Phedron. We shall have Hillmen scouting that trail beginning tomorrow, so that by the time we march we shall know the strengths and dispositions of any guards or patrols before we reach them.

"I will wish you to take the main road, leaving three days after us, and marching quickly. If you meet more than you think yourself able to face in battle, retreat and then draw back into your own land until you can cut them down by raids and ambushes. But you have no need of that advice. Let me ask, though, that if you find yourself unavoidably late, you will send me word so that I will not be depending on your help, and it not be coming."

"Milord, there're men among your force and mine would make high and fearsome oaths about coming or dying in the attempt. I will say no such thing, having seen somewhat of warfare, but will say that if the thing is possible for flesh and blood, I will do it. I can promise no more."

"And I would ask no more," answered the Prince.

TWO WEEKS LATER, Conel led eighteen hundred infantry and two hundred cavalry out. Three days later, they destroyed a twenty-man patrol of Hygerians which had been discovered by the Icarian scouts. In another day, they were turning down the old trail toward Hardinian. It took one whole day and half of another to traverse that section of road, so overgrown was it with brush and shrubbery. Several times, it was necessary to halt the whole host in order to clear a section enough to allow them to pass through.

When they came at last into the settled plain around Hardinian, they were met by several of the local people, from whom they heard news that a large force of Hygerians had just gone up the road to meet with Phedron, while another was gathering just two days' march to the south.

Chapter Twenty

Hardinian had an ill name. When Chaldin raised his revolt, Coerl held in Hardinian, his capital, until it was clear the local people were rather on the side of the rebels. He withdrew to the tiny village of Fwil Don and was given the time he needed for the reorganization of his forces by the fact that Chaldin's men, against orders, paused to loot and burn the city. This act turned many against Chaldin, which he felt sorely at the final battle by Jarth Cliff.

But although Hardinian was rebuilt, and indeed regained much of its old glory, Coerl declared Don to be his new capital, and its name became, through popular use, the City of Coerl.

-History of Asbaln
Horagon

The garrison within Hardinian was little more than five hundred, but the force to the south numbered almost three thousand. Another three thousand had gone northward to meet Phedron, so Conel could expect little help from him immediately. Phedron must almost certainly withdraw back into his hills, being outnumbered by about two to one, and Conel must retreat as well. The force to the south was, by all reports, expected to be at Hardinian within three days.

"How," asked Rorick, "did the two thousand Hygerians between Phedron's Hold and Hardinian become upwards of six thousand?"

"Perhaps someone miscounted." replied Conel, "But the question *we* must ask is this: Do we attack Hardinian or retreat?"

"I would ordinarily say retreat," said Rorick thoughtfully.

"Except," interrupted Conel, "that if we go up the main road, we finish by being caught between two forces, each of which outnumbers us greatly, and if we go up the old track, they will be striking at our rear-guard all the way, while they can easily send word to the other force to cut off our retreat."

"My thoughts precisely," said Rorick. "It seems there is one choice; we must take Hardinian and hold it until Phedron can relieve us. I would say it will be fairly certain when the word goes out that we have captured the city, the Hygerians will most certainly gather against us, leaving Phedron with an almost free hand in the north."

"Two thousand of us against six thousand? You believe it is possible?"

"I believe we can make it possible. Look, we have driven them from across the Mountains so swiftly that they are still surprised. We have come over the Mountains ourselves by a pass they knew nothing of. We are now in the midst of the territory they still hold, and that fact will make them think and wonder what our plan is. That in itself may give us a day or two."

"A message must go to Phedron at once, then, informing him of what we intend, and what we wish him to do."

"Of course."

"And one more thing. Do we take this city before the army to the south of us comes up? Beating on the walls with our fists will not suffice."

"No, that is true. Let us speak to the Old One; he produced the ideas of the stone-throwing engines, and perhaps he will have an idea here. Perhaps I ought to have brought back some of that stuff from the pass, the liquid which melts away rock."

When the Old One heard what the problem was, he said, "I think perhaps an engine larger than those we have already built would suffice, if there are any weak points in the walls of the city. Gather some work-crews if you will, and I will take a few of my colleagues to see to the rest."

BY EVENING, the new catapult was ready. It was enormous, and it was powered by a giant box at the end of the throwing beam which, when it was to be set up, would be filled with rocks and earth. The throwing arm, when this box was hoisted into the air, would lie on the ground, where a large rock was loaded onto it. The loaded box was let fall, and swung the throwing arm up to where it contacted a cross-beam, and released its missile.

The weight of that missile and its range depended mostly on the weight of material in the box. It was a matter of finding the strongest wood, then making the machine strong enough to throw heavy rocks a long distance, but not so strong as to beat itself to pieces in the first few casts.

The Old One took Rorick and Conel out in order to show them where it should attack the wall. "It cannot be seen from here, unaided, but if you mark that patch where the stonework is a little paler? In that area, the wall is badly cracked inside. It has nothing to do with the colour, save it will make a decent aiming point for the catapults. I would be more happy if we had time and materials to produce two or more catapults for this task, but even for one, we shall find ourselves hauling large stones from quite a distance before we are done. I have taken the authority to set men and horses to hauling up such stones already."

"What sort of gap do you expect to make?" asked Rorick.

The Old One shrugged. "Milord, I could throw two dice, add the numbers on their faces, and be as close as would be by any method. It depends on so many things. How long will we have to work? What weight of stones will we find? How many times will we find ourselves deceived by the weight of a stone so it goes too far or too short and does not hit the proper place?

"Let us say that, with good fortune, we will make a gap of fifty feet. With less luck, we may have only five feet. Does that help you?"

Conel chuckled. "So, Old One, we have shown we do not know your business any better than you know ours. We will trust you, then. Will you have a gap of any sort by mid-morning tomorrow?"

"If the Powers smile, we will have a fair by then. You will not want too large a breach, since you be defending the city yourself for some days."

"That is true. When you have achieved this task for us, you must put your mind to methods whereby we can lessen the effect of the breach once we are inside."

"As to that, have already given some thought to the matter, and will consider it even more. We shall have answers for you."

IT WAS EVENING, and around several hundred campfires the men of Asbaln ate, rested, gossiped, and sang. and Conel stood with the Old One near the large catapult, watching as several men strained at the winch which hauled the throwing-arm of the catapult downward. At the same time, some others were manhandling a huge rock toward it.

Then, when the sling at the end of the arm was spread on the ground, the rock was levered onto it, and everyone stood back. A man heaved on a light line attached to the hook and eye mechanism which held the arm down, and it came free. The arm blurred as it whipped upward, and a moment later, they saw where the stone struck on the edge of the light patch. The men cheered and prepared for another shot.

The Old One looked at the Prince and the Guardian. "We have begun. We can continue at this the whole night, and expect to have some results by morning."

"In the darkness?"

"Our stones are generally of a similar weight, so they will, for the most part, strike in the same general area. So long as we keep the machine in its position, we need not fear missing the general area. And it may serve to keep the Hygerians awake and alert all night, to the detriment of their battle-skill tomorrow."

They continued to discuss this and other matters, and suddenly the catapult launched its second stone. This one struck just a few feet above the previous one. "There is no sign of damage," said Conel, "only a few chips of stone and a handful of dust."

"It is too soon to hope for visible results. Come again at dawn, and we can mere you happier."

Later, as the Prince and the Guardian strolled away, Rorick said, "I will take the warriors through the gap to open the gate."

Conel shook his head. "Not this time, my friend. Your Warriors opened the gates of Orden, and those of Avantir. Shall a King hold back while others risk all danger to give him back his kingdom? I will take two hundred men through the gap, and do you have others ready to come through front? The gate is opened."

"So shall it be, then. A good night to you, Conel, and we shall meet in the morning." Rorick walked away to find Beran.

Beran was with the armourer, seeing to the patching of his war-shirt There the rings had worn dangerously smooth. "Beran, the Prince will lead the attack into the city tomorrow. Find Artir and see to it that ten good men are sent along to stay beside him at all times. We can afford to lose battle, but we cannot afford to lose the Prince."

"I would send Dolon to lead them. He is among the best of our young ones, and I have marked him to take my place when the time comes."

Smiling, Rorick shook his head. "I fear this task is not for us, Beran. Conel is too likely to recognize any of the Warriors, and I fear what his pride might lead him to if he felt that he were being guarded as a child."

Beran nodded. "It shall be done, Milord."

As Rorick walked away, he heard a song coming from one of the many campfires, a song which brought to him thoughts and memories of Carill Don.

"The blackbird sings on the broken branch,

The Wind of the night is chill;

I rest alone, but for my sword, Alone on the side of the hill.

Thumill's famed rings, were they mine to give,

I would give, with Andrythn's stone,

Or catch the moon with silver cords To be with my love, alone."

Chapter Twenty-One

The Hygerians learned only very slowly how to deal with walled cities. From the outside, they tended to continue to send men against the walls until the defenders were too few to hold them. On the inside, they usually left them to be held by a very few men, preferring to set their armies outside, and crush their enemies in open battle.
-The Hygerian War
Randell of Avantir

In the morning, they found that a section of the wall had fallen about the width of a small door. While the army was taking its places, the great catapult continued to cast its missiles. Even as they watched, another giant piece, about five feet in width, fell away, and more rock tumbled down before the engine was prepared to cast its next stone. By the time the host was assembled and orders passed, there was a gap of about twenty feet in the wall, with the remains of the wall standing no higher than four feet at the highest.

Rorick looked at the host and grinned. It was still rather a tatterdemalion force, and the bulk of the arms and armour were captured from the Hygerians. There were more of them now, but they still presented the look of a chance-gathered mob. There were even some who had no armour at all and were armed only with a bundle of light throwing spears and a dirk. But they, too, would find a part to play.

Rorick strolled over to join Conel where he was steading with the two hundred men chosen to follow him. Three light catapults were being moved into position so that they could shoot over the heads of the attackers. Rorick spoke:

"Walls crack and crumble; see the white dust rise!

And now the Dragon of Asbaln flies!"

Conel answered:

"Behold, the war-host's trumpet calls;

Forward, then, through the broken walls!"

Rorick withdrew. He cast a quick eye over Conel's two hundred men. They were, for the most part, young men, fierce and eager, and he felt a sadness for which he could not find a reason. Beran spoke suddenly at his elbow. "They are young, and the fire burns fiercely; and of them who will remain to tell to his grandchildren of this day?"

Conel drew his sword, and a trumpet sounded. The three catapults fired, one at a time. They were not so difficult to reload as the large one which had battered down the wall, so they fired quickly, and one was always ready to fire. A hundred archers moved in formation behind Conel's men, and as they drew within range, they began to loose their arrows.

Even with this support, Conel's detachment lost several men to arrows and javelins from the wall, and as they clambered over the rubble in the breach, more arrows and javelins came from behind it. Then the last of them were over the breach and into the city. Clearly, the Hygerians could not mount an effective opposition behind the breach, but from the noise within, the battle was going harder.

Rorick gave a signal to Artir, who took five hundred men forward with twenty ladders. They did not catch the Hygerians completely by surprise, for by the time the ladders were going up against the walls, the numbers of people visible above had doubled. The Icarians who had supported Conel's charge were now supporting Artir, and the result was at least a minor foothold on the wall.

Rorick watched as, for what seemed a terrible length of time, the battle hung in the balance. The small foothold on the wall remained small, there being room for only limited numbers, and the Hygerians were attacking them with fierce determination. It was no longer possible to make any guesses at the state of the battle within, where Conel sought the gates, but Rorick was ready for either of two choices.

He looked at Beran, who was watching Artir's men on the wall with a deep frown of concentration, as though by willing it he could cause them to clear the wall of defenders. "In a moment, we must move. Artir is making no headway, though he *is* drawing them off as we had planned. Either Conel will open the gate, and we will go in by that way, or we will enter by the breach to rescue Conel."

Even as he spoke these last words, the gates moved.

Drawing the Sword, he searched for those to follow him. "For the King!"

He led them at a run toward the gates.

As they swept into the city, Conel met them. His right arm was gashed from wrist to elbow, and he was lightly wounded on the right thigh, just above the knee. He grinned at Rorick. "Well, my friend, shall we take our stroll through the town?"

"Yes, let us go."

They advanced swiftly, passing through the remnants of the two hundred who had followed Conel, and now fought in a semicircle around the gateway. According to the plan agreed upon, two small detachments of the Warriors moved along the flanks with orders to particularly guard against flanking attacks. The Warriors would advance down the wide main street, while further forces entering behind them would take the other four streets which converged upon the gateway.

Then, down the wide main street, the Hygerians counter-attacked. In mid-rush, they cast their javelins, following which they threw themselves upon the front rank, and broke it. It cost them heavily, for most often they broke it by one man leaping upon an Asbalnian, seeking to grapple with him, while another struck with a sword or axe. However, the front rank was shattered under this impact and those that survived fought alone or in small knots surrounded by the Hygerians, who attempted to break the second rank as well.

They failed, for in breaking the first rank, they lost their momentum, as well as whatever cohesiveness they had possessed.

Rorick found himself fighting back to back with Conel, facing a tossing sea of spears, swords, and axes. It was only moments that they fought thus, though it seemed longer, while the second of the warriors advanced steadily, maintaining alignment, pushing the Hygerians before them. Then, as the second rank passed around and closed before the remnants of the first, Conel and Rorick turned and, leaning on their swords, grinned at each other.

From that moment, the Asbalnian attack was no longer in doubt. A further force had come into the breach, and Artir's men had finally cleared the wall enough to begin leaping down inside. The Hygerians, however, continued to fight with their customary stubbornness, leaving no yard of cobblestone uncontested.

It ended much as the battle of Orden had, though here the hostages who had been taken from among the leading citizens were guarded by men with orders to slay them if any rising seemed about to begin. When the people rose, therefore, they first rescued the hostages; seventeen of fifty hostages were slain, but by then the captive population were raging among their captors.

Of the original five hundred, over three hundred died, thirty surrendered, and the rest fled. In a red sunset, Hardinian returned to its owners.

Chapter Twenty-Two

The division of forces by the Asbalnians before the storming of Hardinian was the classic error, though it must be said that they were working on the information, which showed them as having a slight superiority in numbers. As well, the end result of an army appearing almost from nowhere to attack Hardinian was much consternation among the Hygerians. The fact of the existence of the numerous Hygerian troops prevented the consternation from having the full effect it might have had. Therefore, on top of the first gamble, Conel and Rorick gambled on their ability to hold Hardinian.

—The Hygerian War
Randell of Avantir

The Prince's army, now about seventeen hundred strong, took over the city. Now they had only to wait for Phedron. parties set about putting thin. in order for the defense, for it was necessary not only to hold until Phedron's arrival, but to preserve the host as an instrument fit for further fighting.

A ditch was due outside the breach, and a hedge of sharpened stakes was set into the pile of rabble. A special force of men was set to watch the breach and drilled in certain manoeuvres devised for its defence. Men sweated and strained to haul some of the light catapults up to light platforms which had been built for them on the wall, overlooking certain points most likely to be attacked.

The great catapult was brought inside, and mounted in a courtyard, while all available arrows and javelins were collected and placed in baskets on the walls. A good number of the men of Hardinian offered their service to the Prince, and were accepted. As many as could actually use them were given arms and armour taken from the Hygerians or taken from the dead of Asbaln. For the rest, they took to practicing in the use of bows and arrows, or javelins.

There was much practice with missiles going on. Rorick, who had seen what archers could do, kept his Warriors training as much as could be managed at the use of the bow. They were far below Icarian standards, but even the worst of them could now put an arrow into a man—sized target six times out of ten at a range of one hundred yards. Small scouting forces were out on both the north and south roads, to bring warning of the first approach of Hygerians from either direction.

Three days later, it was reported that the Hygerians were on the way from the south. No word had come in yet from Phedron, but it was hoped that he would make his way through before the condition of the force in Hardinian grew too serious.

None of the leaders of the Asbalnians were too greatly disturbed by the presence among the Hygerians of engines for attacking the walls of the city; it had not been expected that such things would be ignored forever by the enemy, though some of the more gloomy—minded of the ordinary soldiers prophesied doom and defeat until restrained by command of the Prince.

"WE NEED TIME, Conel. Every hour we can buy in which they do not attack us is added time for Phedron to come to us."

Conel drummed his fingers on the table before him and looked at Rorick. "And you, my friend, have found another way to buy us a few hours. I think I may not like this, but tell me."

"I will take out a force of cavalry; we will conceal ourselves back in the woods and come down to raid them in the first night. The next day, we will come back through them and return to the city, doing what damage we may on the way."

The Prince slapped his hand down hard on the table. "I was right! I do not like it! A night attack is a good way to get killed, like as not by your own people. And you will cut your way through them in the daytime? Bah! And what sort of magic charm will keep you and these men invisible while their patrols comb the country—side for you?"

"I might die in a day attack as well. We can cut our way through, particularly if there is a sally from the city at the same time. And as for their patrols, well, I had thought to take us very far from the city, far enough that they would not think of looking for us."

"So you come to the fight on tired horses?" Conel's hand fell on the table, palm up.

"Conel, Conel, do you think I have not thought this through? We might sit here all the night arguing so, and end by doing nothing. Will you give me your leave?"

"Yes, I suppose I shall, though my heart likes it not. If I lose you, lose more than another commander."

"I have no wish to deprive you of my company, Conel, but I have a feeling that we may buy some time this way, and time we most desperately need."

THE SMALL GROUP of horsemen met in the brash overlooking the plain round Hardinian. Their scouts drew quick naps in the flickering firelight, showing where all the Hygerian siege equipment was placed. After a quick scanning of the plan, Rorick assigned targets to his men, dividing them into three groups.

They were a hundred, all told, and he felt that thirty was the smallest number which could expect to achieve any success, even by surprise. Each man had a large piece of white cloth tied round his sword—arm, a rough means of identifying comrades in the dimness in which they would be fighting.

They all mounted, and Rorick looked round at them. "No foolishness, now. We are going in to destroy equipment, and if any of you decides to die bravely surrounded by a ring of dead foes, I will personally see to it that a song is made remembering you as a stupid glory—hunter who endangered his comrades by dying when there was no need. Now, let us go."

They rode down toward the Hygerian camp in silence. It had been arranged that the signal to attack would be the challenge by the first Hygerian sentry, and when the voice of a tired man sounded from the darkness before them, they reacted as though a trumpet had sounded.

The sentry's shout brought guard—detachments to the alert, but before they could approach the point of danger, the Asbalnians were splitting into three groups and riding at a gallop for their destinations. They did not stop to fight, though they did ride down several small groups which sought to hinder them.

Rorick's force attacked a large ram, made mostly of green wood and covered with green hides. They had dragged in bundles of brush by means of ropes, and they had several jars of oil with them for just this purpose. They had little hope of actually destroying the ram, but they might possibly make it unusable for some time.

They piled the brush at one corner of the machine, and poured the oil into the same area, then cast in torches. They did not leave immediately, but rather stayed in the neighbourhood for a time, holding back those who would have come to put the fire out.

At last Rorick, noticing that the enemies gathering against them were becoming too numerous, led his men out by the least difficult route, loosing a few arrows on the way against any who attempted to interfere with them.

They stopped first at the place where they had met before the attack. They waited there until as many in as seemed likely to do so, then rode out to a new hiding—place. The Hygerians did not pursue them far.

It only remained to reenter the city tomorrow.

Chapter Twenty-Three

Hardinian stood by the strength of the Sword,
Stood and was held from the dark-haired horde;
Stood like a rock in the raging sea,
That Asbaln's men might be made free.
Icar's arrows, in streaks of light,
Drop, as eagles, from great h*eight;*
Back they drove the western breed,
Standing at bay that their land be freed.
-from "The Holding of Hardinian"
Phedron Double axe

Early in the morning, a pair of men went out to scout the path for them. A little later, the main body left. There were Hygerian patrols, but their scouts warned them well in advance so that they could avoid them. At last, they were in essentially the same position as that from which they had begun their attack the previous night.

Some results of their night's work were visible, the charred areas marking burned stores, the great ram, though not wholly destroyed, canted over at an angle which indicated that it would at least require a good deal of work before it could be made usable again. There was much obvious reorganization going on in the Hygerian camp, and it was some time before any real action began.

The two catapults which remained to them launched their missiles about noon, while men with ropes and ladders formed parties, followed by larger forces immediately behind.

After surveying the approximate form of the assault, Rorick issued some swift orders to his commanders, then mounted. He rode up in front of his force and spoke to them.

"It is not our intention to become dead heroes, fighting gallantly but uselessly among the Hygerian tents this afternoon. We hope to disturb this first assault sufficiently to prevent its having any serious effect on the city, and ourselves enter the city to help fight off further assaults. Anyone who does not do his utmost to reach the city comes very near to committing treason against the King. Now, let us go and give them a day to remember."

He surveyed the faces among the forest of lances. Some were grim, some were smiling, but he felt sure that all would follow him.

At that moment, the men guarding their back-trail came riding in answer to the summons. "Milord Guardian," said one of them, "there is a Hygerian patrol nearly upon us."

"Then it is time for us to be going." He turned his horse and led them over the hill-crest.

All Hygerian eyes were on the advancing attackers, even those who were set to watch for just this eventuality, an Asbalnian attack from the rear. The lesson of last night was learned and had such a highly organized assault on city walls not been such a novelty for Hygerians, Rorick and his force would most certainly have had a more difficult time of it.

Suddenly, the Hygerians turned toward them and were preparing to receive them. Rorick noted with a touch of pride that even as the Hygerian arrows and javelins struck, the line of his cavalry remained perfectly straight. But by this time they were close enough, and the trumpet sounded at his signal, and the whole force broke into a gallop.

The Hygerians had not assembled an effective defence, and Rorick led them at a point where the Dark Ones were still somewhat disorganized. They crashed through the wavering line and watched it disappear. They did not hesitate, but rode directly toward the gate, ignoring the several groups of men who sought to cut them off.

The Hygerian assault force, immediately aware of the shouted warnings and pounding hooves behind them, turned. They were ridden down, and as the Asbalnians struck, many of them fled in all directions. At the same time, the gate of Hardinian opened.

From the gate came all the cavalry available to the Asbalnians, riding to strike into the confused Hygerians and allow Rorick's force to enter safely. Behind them came a powerful force of infantry who formed a semicircle in front of the gate, waiting.

Rorick and his force, not pausing at all, rode directly toward the gate. When they were free of the Hygerian lines, a trumpet sounded the recall, and the rest of the cavalry withdrew behind them. The semicircle of infantry waited until all had entered, watching lest some Hygerians be alert enough and organized enough to try for the open gate. Then the infantry withdrew as well, and the gate was shut.

For three days, while their cavalry patrols combed the countryside for miles, the Hygerians tried only limited assaults, feeling for weakness in the defences. Twice, the Asbalnians sent out small forces to cause consternation and destroying equipment, and this apparently caused the Hygerians to think very hard before simply launching a mass attack.

ON THE THIRD DAY, there was a sudden uproar in the Hygerian camp, and the defenders of Hardinian saw a column of about sixteen hundred men coming in from the north. There were signs of a fairly recent battle, for some of them still wore bandages, but there was obvious rejoicing in the Hygerian camp, especially after there was time for the newcomers to pass their news.

Conel and Rorick stood together on the walls, watching.

"There is a feeling upon me that Phedron has been defeated," said Conel. "And if that is so, then we are indeed doomed."

Rorick could only nod. He considered the idea of attempting to break out, to flee with what they could to the north. Suddenly, out beyond the Hygerian camp, there was a flicker of movement.

A mounted man burst forth from the edge of the woods, and as he did so, a roughly made standard burst free upon the staff he held, a double-bladed axe, red, on a green field. "Look!" he pointed, and Conel looked as well.

Then Rorick leaned down and called to one of the men below, "Find Garth, by the stables, and have him prepare a sally! There is a messenger from Phedron coming in!"

The Hygerians had still not sighted the man, though by now he was crossing the line where the sentries had been posted. As he rode among the tents, shouts of alarm rising among the cheers and cries of joy could be heard. Belatedly, Rorick turned to Conel, "Call up some archers!" He himself turned and ran to the nearest catapult, where the crew were looking over the wall with interest.

"Prepare to shoot! Hurry, we must bring this man in!"

Then, unable to do anything but watch, he clenched his hands on the rough stone of the wall, watching as the man galloped on, bent low over his mount, through a sudden hail of javelins which, miraculously, left him untouched. Mounted men were riding now, both in pursuit, and to head him off, and it was clear that most of them had fresher horses.

Rorick muttered, "Come on, man, come on!" He had passed through the camp, and was nearing the point where the catapult might reach. But a strung out line of galloping Hygerians was about to ride in front of him. Rorick pointed at them and turning to the catapult men when he heard the snap of the string and looked back just in time to see the end of the missile's flight.

The foremost of the Hygerians went down with his horse, and the rest were just far enough back to be forced to turn and pursue the messenger. By the time the catapult was re-cocked, arrows were flying from the archers on the wails, and again the nearest pursuer went down. The catapult snapped again, and Rorick saw earth leap as it struck off to the side. He glanced over at the men on the catapult, and one of them was glancing at him. The man smiled ruefully and shrugged. "One can't be so lucky at all times, Milord."

By then the sound of clattering hooves on cobblestones was heard, and shouts behind them. The gate swung open to let Garth and a hundred horsemen sweep out. By some minor miracle, the archers had prevented the Hygerians from laying a hand on the messenger, but his horse was obviously weary, running now mostly on will, and the mass of men behind hill were coming up, too many for the archers to deal with any certainty, especially as they neared their quarry.

Garth and his men reached the messenger at the same time as the pursuers finally did. The Hygerians, neither in formation for battle nor desiring to fight one, fell back, fighting at first, then fleeing. Garth and his men were not out to fight either, and when they had achieved this purpose, they turned and trotted back to the gate.

THE MAN HAD suffered only a minor shoulder wound, and was brought to Conel and Rorick at once, when his shoulder had been bandaged.

"We met them eight miles south of Relyn crossing, Milords. An early patrol of ours met a Hygerian patrol, and we moved up in battle order, not truly knowing each other's strength. Phedron tried to break through the centre with two squadrons of cavalry, with infantry following. He had practically succeeded at that when the rest of the enemy came up. There were enough of them then that, even after having reinforced their centre, they were able to circle our flanks. Phedron himself led his cavalry to beat back the circling forces on the one flank while the rest of the army was disengaged and fought so fiercely in the rear-guard that the Hygerians pursued not at all.

"We were defeated, but not destroyed. The Hygerians were content to leave a small force to watch Relyn crossing, but neither were we immediately able to seek further battle.

"We received your message the next day, but Phedron says it is not possible for him to come now, and he suggests you return to the hills to meet him there."

When the messenger had been dismissed, Rorick looked at Conel, and Conel returned the look. "Well, Rorick, can we fight our way out of the city to Phedron's Hold?"

"We can, but we will lose a quarter or more of our force in doing so, especially as they will now be expecting some such attempt. And it will be a running fight all the way, so that food would be whatever we could pick up on the way, and we would be scattered and vulnerable. If eight hundred of us reached Phedron, I would say that the Powers themselves were smiling on us."

"And I would estimate that we can hold the city for weeks, and not much more. A week and a half beyond, using every trick we can invent, and perhaps conscripting citizens, but further than that, we must have the luck of Thumill of the Three Rings to survive."

Rorick nodded. "My thoughts as well. And we will need Thumill's luck."

"And. he died, holding fast to his position as well, did he not? You will support my decision to stand here, then?"

"Indeed. I may be wrong, and an attack from here with all our strength might scatter them enough that the most of us might escape, but to be driven a second time from Hardinian might lose for us some part of the faith of the people. Give us a land yet half free in the winter, and by next spring the men of Asbaln might be a little less open of hand toward their still enslaved brothers.

"I think we must hold, though this is not Dwyllen Lhor, and though we wait only for the coming of Phedron and not for the gathering of the Elder Host. May the Powers who smiled on Thumill smile also on us."

A breathless messenger dashed in. "They are coming, Lords!"

Rorick looked at him calmly. "Thank you. Be sure that the men on the walls have been warned. The Prince and I will come out soon, but we have some plans to complete. If the situation becomes more than the Captains on the walls can deal with, send for us again."

The man gave them a surprised look, then he said, "It shall be done, Milord." He strode out, and Conel looked questioningly at Rorick.

The Guardian smiled. "You and I have been engaged, one or the other or both of us, in almost every skirmish fought since I came to you in the Hills. What will the men think if, now, under what seems to be the heaviest attack we have ever suffered, we feel that it is not vitally necessary for us to be on the walls?"

Light dawned in Conel's eyes. "If the situation is such that we do not feel that the Captains of the walls need our presence, why it cannot be so desperate as it seems, can it?"

"Precisely. And when that word is spread to the men, as I am sure that it will, it will be worth an extra five hundred swords on the wall. And since I did say that we must make plans, let this be one! No matter how desperate the situation becomes, we must leave matters to the Captains. We must see to it that the times when we actually step in and draw swords are those times when the fate of all lies in the balance."

Conel nodded. "Yes, there is truth in that. And will it be, I think, long before it becomes absolutely necessary for us to be constantly ready upon the walls. But we must not fail to be seen."

IN A SHOUTING MOB, the Hygerians came up the slope to the city. Their few archers launched arrows, and when the ranged shortened, the others paused to hurl javelins, a seemingly unending stream of them. Though some shafts found their marks, men were falling in the dark-clad ranks as well, for the Icarians were plying their trade, and the Asbalnians had large stocks of Hygerian javelins to use up. Not all those on the walls were expert, or even experienced, at casting javelins, but nearly all were willing to try, and even a beginner may have luck.

The main attack was directed at the breach, of course, and though the ditch and the stakes slowed and hindered them, they did not stop the rush. But in the slowing, they were harassed by arrows and javelins from the breach and from the walls flanking it. Those who managed to pass the stakes set in the rubble of the breach were met by a counter-attack that halted them, and missiles continued to strike into those crowded up behind them.

At other places, ladders and ropes with grappling-hooks were cast up against the walls, but with little success. Eventually, they withdrew. They did not come again until midmorning of the next day.

This time, those in the lead brought up bundles of brush which they cast into the ditch, making the crossing somewhat easier. This time, however, more archers were waiting, and a hundred men were crouched inside, just behind the remnants of the well. Rorick stood back, watching.

In spite of the arrows, numerous enemies managed to come over the wall. As they came down over the precarious footing of the scattered stones, they met the men inside, in three ranks. Rorick watched the hammering, shouting battle as it went, but took no actual part himself. When the Hygerians retreated again, he strolled over to the men in charge of the force. "Well done. You know how it is to be done now. If you have any questions, or if you have any ideas, see me later in my quarters."

"Thank you, Milord." Pride and pleasure showed in the young men's eyes.

But Conel and Rorick were much less unconcerned when together. Alone, they discussed their casualties. "We have lost too many. At this rate, we cannot possibly last until Phedron comes." Conel was frowning, drumming his fingers on the paper before him on the table.

"Two things. First, many of these lost were those who had no armour, or who were casting javelins while the Hygerians were casting theirs. Secondly, their main attempt to scale the wall came at the point where the citizen volunteers were placed. And while the volunteers were not inexperienced, none of them had seen battle for some time."

"Perhaps we should have moved then when we saw the attack coming at them." He waved a hand. "No, I know, we could not, for they were put on the wall precisely to give them confidence in themselves, and to remove them when they were about to be attacked would have destroyed that confidence. But it worries me."

"Yet they have fought off the enemy by themselves, and we are continuing to drill them. In a week's time, our casualty rates will fall. Have faith, Conel."

Conel smiled. "Yes, perhaps I worry too much."

Chapter Twenty-Four

The holding of Hardinian lived in song and story for long after the Hygerian war was over. The Hygerians almost certainly realized both the possible effect on the Asbalnians if the city fell, and the possible result to themselves if the city held until Phedron could return. They had no illusions about having defeated Phedron for good and all, for they had seen Asbalnian armies leap up from places where the land had been thought to be under complete control, and they had seen those same armies move through the land almost as though they were covered by spells of invisibility.

-The Hygerian war
Randell of Avantir

For six days after, the Hygerians assaulted the walls at least once a day. The Hygerian catapults proved to be of shorter range than the Asbalnian ones, and the Asbalnians knocked two of the Hygerian catapults to pieces. However, the continual firing had loosened the supports under the wall-platform of one of the engines, causing it to fall to the courtyard below, seriously damaging the catapult, injuring one man and killing another.

Under the skilled direction of certain of the Old One's colleagues, the wall on both sides of the breach was specially braced, so the heavier Hygerian catapults achieved little there. By now, however, the Dark ones had set up a series of log palisades within closer range of the walls, behind which their few archers took shelter, along with the lighter catapults.

From behind these shelters, the Hygerians would issue, while the archers shot over their heads. The first of them would be a swarm of light-armed men with a bundle of javelins and a shield. These would clash up and cast their missiles up at the men on the wall, while the heavily armed men with ladders and ropes came up behind.

After the sixth day, they ceased to be so ready to storm the city and were more content with shooting into it with catapults and archers. They extended their wooden palisades, angling them continually forward in a zig-zag fashion, so the storming-parties should not have so far to go under the Asbalnian missiles.

While their force was already large, continual parties of Hygerians rode in and encamped themselves around the city, while by this time the Asbalnians had recruited as many of the townspeople as they reasonably could.

On that sixth night, the Hygerians attempted a night attack. They came fearfully close to success, so much so that by morning the defenders were still fighting to clear them out of a section of the city which they had fortified when they had been cut off from reinforcements. It had been a terrible night, with men too often finding themselves in mortal combat with their comrades.

More by good fortune than by their skill, though with some flashes of insight on Rorick's part which seemed almost magical to the men, they prevented the second groups from coming in to reinforce the first party which had come over the walls in near silence. Though they remained carefully on their guard every night from then on, the Hygerians never attempted another night attack; quite possibly they felt the risk of disaster because of inability to distinguish friend from foe was not worth the gain.

When the situation was restored, save for those Hygerians still trapped inside, Rorick had a hurried consultation with Conel, and they sent young Dolon out to find Phedron.

Though the final casualty returns were not yet in, it seemed likely the Prince's army was now just over twelve hundred, and they could not hold out much longer. Rorick was with Dolon just before he went out over the breach.

"Tell him we must be relieved soon, or we are dead. In three days, expect them to realize our situation, and when they do, they will press harder. Go now, and may the High Ones go with you."

Dolon slipped out silently and was gone in the darkness. Rorick stood there for some time, listening to the far-off sounds of the Hygerian camp, without much hope he could distinguish any distinct sound if Dolon should be caught, but wishing to make himself as sure as possible. Conel was suddenly at his side. "If they catch him, they will certainly let us know. They would prefer the immediate disappointment to the growing feeling that something has gone wrong."

"My feelings as well. But they might decide not to let us know, lest we send out another messenger in his place who might be more successful."

Conel shrugged. "Well, I fear we can count the days of our future here in Hardinian now, and they are few. Eventually, they will have extended their siege-wall so close to the city that they will be able to attack almost unhindered."

"Yes, I fear so. Yet we may still be able to hinder them, by one means or another. Come, let us rest while we may."

IN TWO DAY'S time, the situation became desperate. The Hygerians had been building for some time, and had at last repaired the ram, which Rorick had partially burned on the first night. Because of its great weight, it required many men and beasts to move it, so they brought it up behind their shields. They found the sharp corners which they had put in the palisades made it impossible to turn the unwieldy bulk of the great engine, so they were forced to remove great sections of the palisade.

This delayed them, and they had to leave the ram halfway down the siege-walls over one night, while they rearranged all the corners to allow for it. They had lost somewhat heavily at the previous point, which was only within extreme arrow-range, but was within good range for the catapult nearest it, and so did not wish to make the extra required effort that night. Some said later that it was the unaccustomed work, added to the continual vexation by the missiles, which made it impossible for their officers to drive them to the attack by any means at all.

That night, Rorick led a sortie against the siege-wall, but it was guarded well enough they could not achieve anything significant. There were more consultations between Rorick and Conel, and shortly the catapults shot once more. This time they were launching jars instead of stones, jars which burst against the palisade to scatter oil across it.

Before long, it was drenched with oil, and the catapults then launched burning darts in the same area. The palisades were made of green wood, thus not too likely to burn themselves, but when the oil scattered over that particular section of the siege-wall had burned and the wood suffered as well.

There had been little hope of destroying the wall, or any substantial portion of it, but the heat of the fire prevented the Hygerians from approaching it, which delayed them in bringing up the ram.

Then too, even before the fire died down appreciably, the catapults were launching stones at that part. At the same time, the main gate opened so that the great catapult which had broken the breach in Hardinian's walls began shooting its massive missiles at the palisade. The burning section finally broke, its posts weakened by the fire, and the great catapult sent two large rocks at the ram before the defenders of the city felt it necessary to close the gates.

Despite the vexatious missiles coming from the walls, the Hygerians hauled the past the cap in the palisade. At last, having reached the limits of the siege-wall, they rested again. Then came another attack, an attack aimed principally at the breach, but with diversions towards other areas of the walls.

As the dark-cloaked mob surged forward, Rorick ran to the catapult nearest the front gate. "This is to divert our attention while they bring the ram up to the gate! Wait for them!"

And so it proved. Yet the assaults were aimed at the area of the catapult, and pressed so thoroughly that the catapult crews drew swords to defend themselves, and only managed two shots at those hauling the ram.

A few more braces were added to the already reinforced gate, and as the first assault fell back to the palisades, the Hygerians pushed the great engine into position in front of the gate, while others began hastily setting up new palisades to protect those Who were to operate it. A new line of palisades was also erected to allow their archers a place to shoot from.

The sound of the ram booming against the gate was soon heard throughout the city. Asbaln's men waited until it should give way at last.

It took some time before it fell. In fact, it held until mid-morning on the second day of the ram's placing. As it finally broke and fell, a horde of Hygerians behind the original siege wall offered shouts of triumph. They attacked the gate, the breach, and certain sections of the wall.

But the Asbalnians had not been idle. Inside the gate was a semicircular breastwork, with a light catapult behind it, aimed at the gate. Archers stood all around it, with parties of swordsmen standing just a little back from it to allow the bowmen full room for their occupation.

The top of the rubble in the breach had been smoothed, and a breastwork set up there as well, with archers behind it, and spear-men and swordsmen to support them. The Hygerians found themselves with a task only slightly easier than before the cate had gone down.

But they were determined, and the fact the gate had gone down had heartened them, and it seemed hours before they withdrew. They had done better on the walls, two hundred of them actually making their way over the walls, and forcing on too far, to find themselves cut off from any hope of reinforcements. While the noise of that fight was still ringing over one pact of the city, the city's defenders made further preparations.

Men, mostly those of the wounded who could yet walk, were going round the city collecting what arrows and javelins they could find to augment the supplies available on the walls. A hasty barricade was thrown up across the gateway, and manned first archers, with swordsmen behind them. breastwork behind the gate-way was also manned, and they prepared to fight.

The Hygerians came once more that day, and were driven back again, though not easily. The men of Asbaln had an uneasy night, but the Hygerians had no intention of risking a night attack. In the morning, though, they came again.

The breastwork at the gate was far enough in being beyond the reach of the Hygerian ram, so they launched an assault on it with only some help from their catapults. The barricade, being hastily constructed, did not stand well against this treatment, but it protected the men behind it to some degree.

When the dark-clad men came to close quarters, the Asbalnians met them with a grim ferocity. Conel directed the fighting at the gate. Rorick supervised the walls; there was no more pretence at unconcern, for every man knew their situation was desperate.

The Hygerians knew it too and were a shade too confident in their first attack. They drove the Asbalnians back from the barricade but were then subjected to arrows and javelins in a deadly crossfire from the circular defence within. At the breach, which they had some time ago discovered was not the easy entrance it as looked to be, their attack was only enough to ensure that the defenders must maintain their full alertness there as well, keeping several hundred men occupied.

Again they withdrew, but it was clear they would come again and again, and soon it would no longer be possible for the defenders to prevent them from gaining a foothold in the city, and that would be the beginning of the end.

Rorick, leaning on the Sword and watching as the men of Asbaln made preparations for the next attack, realized that Hardinian must fall, and with it, it seemed, the hopes of Asbaln. Yet perhaps... He went down off the wall to find Conel.

"Milord, you must escape."

"And desert the war-host? I cannot, you know that, Rorick."

"Milord, if I die, if Artir dies, if Phedron dies, then another commander may take our place. But you are the last of the Royal Line of Asbaln, and if you die, the country dies."

Conel looked down at his feet, then back at Rorick. "As always, Rorick, you speak the truth, though I like it not. Let us wait until dark, then, and make a sudden attack. We may drive right through them, then split into small bands and mere for the hills, each man for himself. Will that satisfy you?"

"It must be so. Clearly the best time for such a sally is after dark, and clearly our best hope for any to escape is to send out the whole of the host. Tell the men we must hold only until dark; it will give them something to fight for, to know that the length of the struggle is limited."

The alarm sounded, and Rorick went back to the wall. Halfway up the stair, he turned and saluted the Prince.

"Asbaln's men were stubborn ever."

"And Asbaln's Kings more stubborn still."

Now came the war-shouts and whistling arrows, the ladders thumping against the wall, grappling hooks grating on stone. Then the ring of steel on steel. Throughout the clanging, shouting din, Rorick strode with the Sword in his hand.

"Hold firm, lads, hold fast, hold hard. Only until dark, then we need hold no more. Stand, now, stand for the sun goes down; hold them back until nightfall. Have courage, men, for the sun is falling, and still we stand. Behold, the sun goes to rest, and yet we hold firm."

The barricade at the gate held firm, though the Hygerians piled their dead before it with reckless abandon. When Rorick once looked to the breach, he saw the defenders there were growing fewer, while the dark tide of attackers washed over them. Around the walls he strode, and when he next looked, the breastwork had fallen.

Even as he watched, a small band of Icarians loosed lighted arrows toward the dark mass. Suddenly, at various points, sparks of light appeared, small bright buds which soon blossomed orange. The wood of the breastwork had been soaked with oil in several places, and the wood was dry enough in any case. In the winking of an eye, the whole of the breach was filled with flames which trapped those already inside and prevented those outside from reinforcing them.

Soon, Rorick was called back to his own task of maintaining the defence of the walls. He was in the midst of leading a counter-attack at a band of about thirty, which had found footing on the wall, when he was dimly aware of Hygerian war-horns calling insistently. Then, almost suddenly, there was not a live Hygerian within reach.

Leaning on the Sword and breathing heavily, Rorick looked out across the valley, conscious of the swelling murmur around him, and saw an army coming out of the brush. Above their heads, the Red Dragon of Asbaln moved sinuously in the wind.

The first group of infantry had come out, moving rapidly into formation, with five hundred cavalry taking position on the flanks, and they moved forward even as the rest of the infantry were forming behind them.

Commanding the force was a big man on a gigantic horse, his helmet decorated with the wings of a white mountain eagle; suddenly men in the city were shouting "Phedron! Phedron Doubleaxe!"

Now the cavalry was well in motion, and the manner of their riding, if such evidence were needed, showed them to be highlanders of the north. The first group of infantry, which proved to be the smaller, moved forward at a rapid pace, maintaining its formation, while the second group, directly under Phedron, moved a little slower.

It could be seen now that the Hygerians had not been taken completely unawares by the advance of Phedron, for there were groups formed and ready to meet him, swift bands of cavalry riding in to harass them with javelins and ride away, while infantry were falling into ranks. Because they were somewhat spread round the city, and they had been very much involved in their assault on the city when the word had reached them, it was taking them a little time to form their front. That they were not immediately crushed was due mostly to the fact that Phedron's host had required some time to move out of the brush.

Even so, it was not long before bands of Hygerian infantry were circling the flanks and rear of the foremost infantry force, while the cavalry, having crushed several formations of infantry, were forced to fight a melee battle with a numerically superior of Hygerian horsemen. At this point, two things happened; firstly, the men in the city came to their senses and prepared to go out to their comrades, and secondly, the bulk of Phedron's infantry, the force coming up behind under his personal command, bolted forward like hounds unleashed in the sight of their quarry.

Their formation became ragged. In some places, their lines disappeared in a surging mass of men, but they fell on the bands of barbarian infantry and annihilated them.

It took a little time for the men in the city to come out, for they had blocked the gate very well, but come out they did. The enemy, seeing themselves as too scattered to fight against both forces, withdrew along the road leading to the City of Coerl.

The men of Asbaln pursued them no further than to send them on their way, for the men of the West were protected in their retreat by a rear-guard, dour men, grim-faced and bitter-handed.

Afterward, Phedron rode into the city to where Conel sat beside the date, on the remnants of the hastily dismantled breast-work receiving reports from his captains. The Prince, who had suffered several minor cuts in the past few days while defending the city, had gained a few more wounds today, all of them now bandaged. Clearly weary, he still greeted Phedron with warmth. The Northerner was not himself unscathed, for the left side of his long yellow beard was red from a wound at the rim of his helmet while his left arm was laid open from wrist to elbow. The great double axe was still in his right hand, but he had cast his shield aside earlier when it had been battered until it was unserviceable.

"Milord King, I bring you an army. I regret my tardiness, but there was little help for it."

"But what matters, Phedron my friend, is that you did come in time. And I note your host is somewhat larger than previously. How did you manage this?"

Phedron shrugged. "It was clear we had need of numbers, so I set to recruiting. We went to each farm and holding with the words, 'Let one man in three come with us, lest the Hygerians burn the steading.' When that failed us, we said, 'One man in three, or we burn the steading.' though we smiled as we said it, none forced us to light torches."

"Will that not add to my difficulties after the war?"

Phedron chuckled, "In the hills, we have a saying: 'two things are not to be criticized; a mother's new baby, and a victorious King.' When all is over, remit a few taxes; they will hail you as greater than Conel the Wild.

"But, to continue, I did not wish to trust them, the new men, to hold to their ranks as the veterans would, for we could not give them the training we would have wished, but set some veterans among them and kept them behind the trained men. I fear my captains are hoarse from keeping them in line, but they did right well out here when I slipped the leash. And they will do well enough when the time comes to fight again, now that they have had their first taste.

"And, without a doubt, they are now the bravest of veteran warriors in their own minds, having seen the enemy flee before them. Ah well, think we fight one more battle. They will feel that they must defeat us; Hygeria is in turmoil, and losing faith in King Razak. That will be the final trial."

PHEDRON'S MEN took over all the defence of Hardinian, as well as patrolling and recruiting. The recovery of the larger cities, Orden, Avantir, and Hardinian, had supplied enough for the pay-chest of the army, with some over. By the best of luck, men loyal to the Prince had been at the discovery of the largest hoards of Hygerian loot, so a good number of these went to the war-chest. Recruiting was made somewhat easier, knowing that men could count on being paid.

They now had about forty-five hundred men. They had about seven hundred and fifty cavalry, two hundred Icarian archers, one hundred fifty of the Guardian's Warriors, and the remainder ordinary infantry, most with sword, shield, and armour, though some still went to battle bearing a bundle of javelins.

They discovered as well, how it was that the Hygerians had more men between the Relyn and Hardinian than had been originally thought. It appeared that Razak had used all his authority and whatever powers of persuasion he possessed to convince the Hygerians he could indeed subdue the Asbalnians, providing he was given the troops to do so.

They had furnished the troops, though not gladly, and when Phedron had been forced to withdraw from the crossing of the Relyn, it seemed Razak could fulfil his promise.

With this, and with the line's force being shut up in Hardinian, certain Hygerian lords volunteered forces which were not asked for, seeing the possibilities for aggrandizement in a reconquest of Asbaln.

"But we have spoiled all that," said Artir to the council.

"I wish it were so easy," said Conel.

Rorick nodded. "They did not suffer exceptional losses when Phedron arrived. They realized soon enough that they were not in a position for a proper battle, and withdrew, preserving the greater part of their force."

"And Razer can tell his council that they have shown, at the crossing of the Relyn, that they *can* match us. It is not over yet."

Phedron stroked his beard as he spoke. "But I think we will have as much time as we need to complete the training of our men before we fight again."

Chapter Twenty-Five

Much care did the leaders of Asbaln take to select the best field for the final battle. It must be one where the tactics which they had practiced and almost perfected could be usefully employed, and yet one where they could be fairly sure of the Hygerians actually coming to them. They desired a feature to protect at least one flank, and yet one where they could put a good number of men into the first line of battle. They settled at last on the plain between the Cliffs of Jarth and the Dark Forest of Chaldin. There, both flanks were secure, and yet a reasonable line could be formed.

-The Hygerian War
Randell of Avantir

They waited at Hardinian for some while before they marched, and even then, they did not move too swiftly. They had been hearing for some days of a gathering of the enemy at the City of Coerl, but neither scouts nor spies seemed able to say much beyond the fact they were there in great numbers. Razak had made a declaration.

'No more shall we send out a few men to deal with these. No longer shall small bands go forth, nor meagre bands set out. Let all the warriors gather, let each mighty man come in; your King shall take the lead, and your Lord ride before you.'

Estimates of the total force available to Razak varied between six and eight thousand, depending on the estimator's consideration that the Hygerians had not had notable success in battle since Dryx Ford. It was true that Razak himself had not come to battle since, considering the paltry forces arrayed against them to be unworthy of his attention.

At first, defeated commanders who survived the battle were executed on King Razak's orders, but realization eventually came that the fault was not theirs. The commander who had met Phedron at the crossings of the Relyn, and was later driven from before Hardinian, a man named Sharakh, was not even completely removed from the King's favour. Previously styled 'Favoured Companion of the King,' he was now allowed only to call himself 'Friend of the King,' and was allowed only twenty retainers in place of his previous hundred.

Yet Sharakh remained as supreme Commander under Razak; though of no greater status would take his orders directly, Razak listened closely to his advice, and no man disobeyed the king's orders.

Steep, black, forbidding, the Cliffs of Jarth brooded over the green plain, above the encamped any of Asbaln. They were unclimbable on the eastern side, save for the Notch, the place where they had crumbled long ago to form a gentle slope up to the grassy incline of the western side.

***Here follows the tale of the Cliffs*:**

In a time long past, Clan the King of Asbaln had twin sons, Codal and Jarth. Codal was but minutes the older, and a constant rivalry had grown up between them, and each felt better able to rule the land than his brother, each also having little thought save for his own desires. Both had an ability to sway the minds of men, so at the death of Olan, the land was ablaze, turmoil and contention riving its accustomed peace.

Three times signs were sent to the two antagonists, portents from the High Powers, that they should forgo this war and make peace. But Codal swore an oath when wise men would counsel him, saying,

"The High Powers rule in heaven, but I upon the earth."

Jarth also rejected advice, saying, "If the Powers could do aught, they would remove my brother, who is unfit to rule; since they have not done this, what then can they do?"

So it was that when the two hosts met for battle, destruction came upon them. Dark night fell in the midst of day, thunder raged and lightning smote, the earth shook, and when daylight returned, the place where the two armies had stood was covered by a cliff of black stone, lying like a scar would where the earth had been wounded.

Yet there had been one among the host of Codal, a man of the Elder Folk whose name was Troyan. Troyan, a man of wisdom and courage, strove until that battle was joined to dissuade Codal from his course. Yet because of the oaths he had sworn, Troyan went forth with sword in hand to the battle line and was lost with the rest.

The brother of Troyan, Lhorannon the Wise, sought long and far, prying into things of difficulty for mortal men, for the answer to a great riddle. After much seeking, he returned to the Forbidden Lands to take his findings to the Elder Council.

Following this, he went to the cliff. It is not known what he did there, though some say he smote on it with a rod, some say with his hand, some say only that he sang a song of strange words. But the cliff cracked and crumbled, and his brother came forth. In that one place, therefore, the cliff was divided, and not the sheer stone surface it presented elsewhere, and there also the grass grew green and fair as on the rest of the plain.

Here, between these cliffs and the Forest of Chaldin, the host of Asbaln took its position.

It was upon the area of the Forest that Coerl had been joined by Arvandal when naught grew there but grass and a few low bushes. Here, bearing the Sword, Arvandal had smitten Chaldin and his rebel barons, smitten them and driven them from the field, so the throne was secured for Coerl.

It was said Chaldin, in the wreck of the battle, as he lay dying, had cursed the land on which he lay, and the result of it was soon seen. Now the forest was dark and thick, a tangle which a man could scarce penetrate, and which few cared to; within it walked were-beasts, and things darker and more difficult to name. Things best not thought on.

SO IT WAS that one flank of the Asbalnian host would be rested upon the Cliff of Jarth, the other on the Dark Forest of Chaldin. If the enemy sought to come over the Notch, then a small force could hold that place for a suitable length of time, hopefully long enough for those below to finish the battle.

"We must keep watch for such a movement," said Rorick. "We can no longer trust to their older tactics of a head-on attack with every man who can be crowded in. We have taught them too much."

"One man atop the cliffs, who can signal us if they come." This was Conel's suggestion.

Rorick nodded. "That will do well enough. We will want all our men to be available on the plain unless they do come through the Notch. If they do not, may well wish for the two hundred or so who would be needed for a permanent guard."

SCOUTS AND SPIES announced the Hygerian force as large beyond counting, at the first. Later estimates set it at something over seven thousand, possibly as high as eight. Host of Asbaln, though slightly grown, was about five thousand five hundred, which was the number they would go into battle with, minus whoever would, between this day and that, suffer some mishap which would make him incapable of fighting. Though much effort and time had been spent in training them, they were still not yet of the quality to inspire glorious feelings of joy in their immediate commanders.

Veterans, this meaning anyone with two battles to his credit, were mainly spread among the newer men to give them both confidence and an example. The most necessary manoeuvres had been drilled into them so much they swore they could perform them while sleeping. Those who trained them swore it was as though they *were* sleeping most of the time when they were attempting to carry out their manoeuvres. Yet they were all confident that, when the time came to open files and allow the cavalry to ride through, not too many would be run down.

ONE NIGHT, THE horizon was red with the light of the Hygerian campfires. On that same evening, Rorick and Conel were discussing various things when the Old One came into their tent. "I must speak with you, Lords." they looked up at him, he continued. "As you may know, it often happens that seeings come to those of my profession, seeings unbidden and unclear. Such a seeing has come, and though we have striven to make all clear, we can discover only certain things regarding this. Three fights will be fought in the coming days, each one providing the reason for the following one.

"Tomorrow's battle, the battle of the armies, is the first. If it is won, then the Black King and the Gold will fight on the steps of the palace stair in Coerl's city. A battle of men it will be, and if it is won, then the third battle follows." He paused.

"And that is...?" encouraged Conel.

"It is difficult to know. A battle comes in a hidden place, where only the Power will determine the outcome, or even the coming out again. So." He spread his hands. "It is little enough, I know, little for help or hindrance, but these three battles must be fought and won before the King may sit on the throne once more."

Conel stood and bowed. "Our thanks, Old One. You have served our cause well, and we owe you much."

"I serve as may, Lord, and as much from necessity as yourself. There appear to be certain magicians of Hygeria, men in high places, who seek to destroy all trace of Asbalnian magic. So intent on this they are, that we are hunted like wolves; our own safety depends on your cause.

"And yet, there is much that is good in the magic of Hygeria. Their healing spells, for instance... But I grow rapidly wearisome when I discuss my own craft. Let it stand that those who were united by the Sword of Conel the Wild are not meant to live peaceably as slaves."

He strode away, tall and erect for all his years. It was then they took note of the clashing of iron across the camp beside one of the fires. Strolling over to see what was happening, they found young Dolon and another fighting with practice swords, wearing their armour, and with padding on arms and legs.

The other man was tall and well-built, making the slender Dolon seem small by comparison, and the two of them moved swiftly and gracefully as dancers. The move which ended the match was so fast as to have been almost invisible; Dolon parried a blow upward, over his head, then struck a return blow to the shoulder. An instant later, the watchers, recognizing a fair hit, set up a shout.

The two men saluted and lowered swords, then the big grim man smiled, a little ruefully. One of the Warriors, noticing Rorick beside bin, grinned and informed him, "Dolon has yet to be bested, and has fought most of the best of our swordsmen."

"I can see his skill, but has he been matched with Beran yet?"

Some of the men around heard this and asked Beran to challenge Dolon. He demurred, but they continued to badger him; he said he was too old for such foolishness, and they declared if he was too old for a friendly match with practice swords, he was too old for going into battle with sharp steel on the morrow. Reluctantly, he prepared. He took his stead, right foot, advanced, sword ready. One of the younger men said to one beside him, "I will wager on Dolon.
"

The other answered, "I will take money from a fool as well as from any other. How much?"

While they and others laid their bets, Dolon lunged from a relaxed stance, and was taken off guard when Beran's sword flicked upward, knocking his blade off its path. He barely kept his balance, and it was only a quick-twisting leap backward which saved his skin from Beran's return blow. He swung a backhand, which Beran also stopped, then as he lunged forward again, the older man went into action.

His right foot slid back, and he shifted his upper body, then stepped forward as the other sword went by his chest.

His own steel shot forward in a thrust which struck solidly against the chest of the younger warrior.

Dolon, too seasoned a warrior not to know that there is always someone better than the best, grinned at Beran, who said in his quiet way, "Twenty years ere you were born, I became a Warrior. For the past ten years, I have trained the newcomers to our ranks. In fact, I gave the Guardian his training, and he is among the best in the kingdom."

The shout was immediately set up. "Let the Guardian and Beran match!" Both demurred, and when the men insisted, Rorick stepped forward and signed for quiet.

"I will not match with Beran, not for any of you. Would you have me look a complete fool, attempting to best the man who has taught me every trick I know, and knows a few more besides? Look elsewhere for your amusement."

"Why then," said a man, "Let the Prince and the Guardian show their skill, one against the other!"

Now at this, the shouting was so loud and insistent the two looked at each other, shrugged and began to prepare. When they had donned the pads and taken up the swords, they circled cautiously, seeking an opening. Twice the swords rang together as they sought openings which appeared for mere moments, and were closed as quickly.

Soon, they were engaged in earnest. The swords flickered and struck, glinting with the firelight, ringing like bells. Back and forward they went, each saving himself more than once by a quick leap forward or sideways. Overall, there was silence, for the men were awed by the skill with which each fought. None could afterward describe the series of movements which led to the end of the bout. They were standing in a lunging position, each with the blunted point of his sword pressed against the other's chest.

Stepping back, they saluted, then lowered the swords. The silence continued until Beran stepped forth to say, "A draw. I will say it, I who stood beside Karkal of the Silver Ring when the Vakon sea-rovers sailed up the Ilcaniar to attack Avantir; such swordsmanship has rarely been seen, and Garthell Longsword of the Elder Legends could scarce have done better. With such leaders, those who come against us shall have no easy fight."

Three loud cheers were given for the King and the Guardian, and the two young men walked back to their tents while the bout was still being discussed animatedly among the rest of the Warriors. "Well, Rorick, the men are in good spirits. What will be helpful tomorrow? Do you think we can win?"

"If we cannot, now is certainly not the time to be worrying over it. We have chosen the ground, and we have made our cavalry, by our tactics, superior to theirs in all but numbers. And our infantry has been better than theirs all along. Given only that luck is not completely against us tomorrow, we will win.

"Tell me, my friend who is always thinking on such things, how have we managed to come so far so quickly? My thought tells me it is our speed which has done it."

"Aye, our speed and the fact we did not fight as we have been used to. In the old times, when they took a portion of our borderland, our hosts marched through in methodical fashion, never passing on until they had cleared every barbarian from the land around them.

"This time, we sat in the Hills, sending out raiding and foraging parties, and they waited until we should begin our movement. One morning, we stood at the gates of Virdan. When we had taken that, they began to prepare for our coming at Orden. Again, we were at Orden, and though they had been expecting us to wear ourselves out against the wells of the city, still we were not expected so soon.

"And Orden, which ought to have held for weeks, went down in one red day of fighting. And while we fought against the land around, they gathered at Avantir where we had stood them off for so long. The sudden fall of Avantir must have seemed a work of magic to them, and it was at that time they surrendered the land east of the Mountains to us.

"But our magic was still strong, and after a few useless assaults on the pass, we were across and joined with Phedron. We have always attacked where we ought not to be, and it is no wonder they worry over what we might do next. Now, we stand waiting on an open battlefield, so they will hesitate to see whether they can sniff out the trick in it. While they are doing this, we shall fight them with an eye for every mistake they make, every instant of carelessness or over-caution, and thereby win the fight."

"Aye. And it has been as you have said. I have heard it said among the men they have spent more time missing meals through forced marches than they have in fighting the enemy."

For a while, they sat in quietness in the tent.

BERAN CAME TO the door of the tent. "Milord. Guardian, I would speak with you in private."

"Certainly." Rorick rose and went out into the night with the old Warrior.

"My Lord, you will know I am of the line of Ralf Starblade, and we mark our beginning with ancestors who fled the Old Island. It may well be you do not know that to the men of our line, it is often given to see when we are to die. My time comes tomorrow, and I may only make ready. I would ask two things, that my sword be taken back to be given to my son, and that you should put Dolon in my place after the battle. He will serve you well."

Rorick stood still and thoughtful. It was hard enough to know many would die tomorrow, but to know that certain ones would certainly die was almost too much to bear. He looked up at Beran and said, "As you request, it shall be done."

They were saved from a long and uncomfortable silence then, for across the camp came the noise of shouting. It was the sound of challenges being shouted from the picket-posts along the edge of the camp next to the Hardinian road, and Beran's sword was in his head as they ran towards it.

In the flickering Light of the torches they found a swelling number of men, armed and half-armed, facing another group of travel-weary men, some mounted, others afoot. Their leader was a large man, somehow familiar, white of hair and beard, wearing a leather war-cap and a chain war-shirt with a recent patch on the chest. Immediately behind was a younger, slighter-built man, similarly armed, but with a metal war-cap his youthful face was close and grim, and his hand rode on his sword-hilt.

Then the older man caught sight of Rorick and as he turned his dancing horse, the firelight flickered on a pattern of silver threads on his scabbard. Recognition flashed to

Rorick as the older man quieted the hubbub with a command which cut through the noise like a naked blade.

"Quiet, then, the lot of you! The Guardian is here, and can recognize me, and assure you I mean no harm." He looked to Rorick, "Perhaps you'd not remember me, sir, but I be Cadda, son of Fannan, son of Brenan, son of Fernmal. We came to you at Virdan.

"What last I heard, Fannan was a leader of ten for the King; Vandinal be at home, wounded in the right arm, so grievous as not to be using it again, that from Avantir Gate. Fannan were left stark dead on the field at Dryx ford, and I were grievously wounded about the chest when we attacked the Pass.

"Having recovered somewhat, I brought away Brioughir and a few neighbours wishful to come along. We gathered a few more on the way, and when we came to Hardinian, they told us you had come up here, expecting one more great battle shortly.

"But when we are arrived, this fellow greets us like we were King Razak and all his armies. So, Lord Guardian, please to tell them who I be, and let us be done with all this, that these lads with me may get to our rest. Tomorrow will be a lively day, I'd wager.

Rorick smiled. "This man is known to me indeed. Come, some of you show them where they may rest, and see to finding food for them. And as Cadda says, tomorrow will be a lively day, so best that all go back, find your places, and rest."

And indeed, in not too long a time, the host of Asbaln was at their rest.

Chapter Twenty-Six

Swift fly darts from Icar's bows
Conel's host to battle goes;
Sword and axe rage through the fray,
Pierce the fight to win the day.
Now the Three hold Asbaln's line,
Steading under the Dragon-sign,
A wall of swords halts Razak's hordes;
Now cry ye woe, Hygerian Lords!
-from "Battle at Chaldin"
Artir One-eye of the Midland Plain

With the morning's light, Asbaln's host took its long-practiced positions. A little later, a great cloud of dust was rising on the horizon, which hid the Hygerian hosts from their view. By mid-morning, spearpoints glinted along the hill, and a long sigh went down the ranks of Asbaln as each man took a deep breath. A dark mass appeared beneath the spearpoints, poured over the rim of the hill, and suddenly the host of Razak faced that of Conel.

Conel, Rorick, and Phedron sat their horses behind the line.

The wind was at their backs, a light breeze, swirling cloaks and stirring Phedron's beard. It would add a little to the range of their bows. Conel spoke:

"Once more the sword, again the spear,

To weapons all, the battle's near.

Once more to strive, then let strife end,

For homeward now our thoughts do tend."

Rorick answered:

"The heart which in the fight was strong,

And from the striving would not cease,

Longs but for that which is the prize;

The victor's crown, the life of peace."

Not to be outdone, Phedron wrinkled his brow, and declared:

"The Seven Hills are shelter sweet,

And may it come to pass,

That I should once more see sunrise

On Homeland's fair green grass."

Then, looking at the other two, he said, "Very pretty. Now let us turn our attention to the crowd over there, so that we may survive to make more poetry"

Indeed, it was not much later that the Hygerians sent in their first attack. No cavalry came forward, but only about two thousand infantry. They did not attempt to engage the entire line, but rather struck in several places along the line, feeling for weakness.

Rorick looked at Conel. “We have let too many of their infantry escape in previous battles; they have learned some good lessons.”

Conel nodded, a trifle morosely. “If we win, we will have earned our victory.”

Asbaln’s archers were not idle, but the infantry who reached the line required, as Phedron put it, “all the killing that could be managed.”

The three of them, leaving the general control of the battle to the lower commanders, rode up and down the line, looking for signs of weakening, encouraging the men. There were, along the line, just behind it, small bodies of reserves intended to retrieve the situation if the line were breached.

One small band of Hygerians, who seemed to have no cares for living or dying, flung themselves at the centre of the line, forcing it to give way. As it stretched first, then broke under the impact, the attackers redoubled their efforts; a further force from the Hygerian lines set out, obviously intent on taking advantage of the break.

Rorick, Conel, and Phedron came together there, and led some reserves in to stop the gap. They advanced slowly but steadily, thrusting back the Hygerians, who were losing some of their initial fervour.

Even so, it was a near thing. They had just restored the line when the reinforcements struck. These, finding no gap to exploit, flung themselves in, intending to produce another. All they managed to do, however, was to hamper each other. Shortly after this, the entire first attacking force was in retreat.

AS THOUGH THIS were a signal, the Hygerian cavalry attacked. The Asbalnian cavalry dashed forward to meet them; those armed with bows rode swiftly toward the foe, turning at dangerously close range to the accompaniment of volleys of arrows, and raced away, shooting as they went.

The Hygerians, pursuing these, were struck by the rest of the cavalry, including Phedron’s lancers, and a swirling melee resulted. Superior training of the Asbalnians eventually overcame the superior numbers of the Hygerians. The Dark ones eventually broke and returned to their own lines.

Chapter Twenty-Seven

After the repulse of their first infantry assault and the following cavalry attack, the Hygerian attempted their flanking manoeuvre. It appears from what evidence remains that Sharakh, who had commanded at Relyn and at Hygerian, saw the opening and brought the force over the Notch. However, even this possibility, though highly discounted, was not entirely unexpected by the Asbalnian Lords. The Warriors of the Guardian had been standing idle all morning, a reserve force intended to deal with such possibilities.

-The Hygerian War
Randell of Avantir

Shortly after this, Rorick was aware of a force leaving the Hygerian main body. Something like a thousand infantry and two hundred cavalry set out around the base of the dark Cliffs of Jarth. It was obvious what they planned; the far side of the Cliff was an easy slope, and the Notch would let them ride directly down into rear of the Asbalnian line.

Rorick looked around. The Warriors were drawn up in ranks a little distance away; some of the younger ones were a bit put out about not being placed in the front line. They were a proud, grim band of men, their clothing and equipment as motley as that of the rest of the host, though all had red cloaks (of nearly the same shade) to set them apart.

He turned to Conel. “Well, they have seen it. Time to go and bar the Notch. See to matters here, and see that you finish soon, for we can hold them for a time, but not forever.”

Conel looked at him, his face grave. “What troops will you take?”

"What troops? My own Warriors, of course. "

"Are they not few for the task?"

"Few enough, but I doubt that we can spare much more from our lines here. As I said, see that you finish soon."

Conel raised his sword in a salute, which the Guardian returned. "May the Powers smile upon you in this fight, then."

Rorick nodded, turned away, riding over to where the warriors waited. "Well," he addressed them, "It seems that you will be able to take in the fight, and somewhat earlier than I had intended. Come on!"

THEY SET OUT at a quick pace, for though they had somewhat the shorter distance to cover, Rorick wished to have some time to pick the most advantageous position for his stand. The fair green grass stood knee-deep on the Notch, and Rorick picked a spot where the ground fell away in a sheer slope on both sides of it, making outflanking the defenders near to impossible.

They formed into three ranks, and Rorick save some general instructions to them. He commanded the front rank, Beran the second, and Dolon the third. A single horseman showed himself on the sky-line, then was gone. "They will be coming now," Rorick said.

It was not much longer before the Hygerians were heard on the other side of the hill, horses stamping, men shuffling, equipment jingling, and low-voiced commands. Then horses began moving, and suddenly, made taller by being silhouetted against the sky, the first ranks of the Hygerian horsemen appeared. As the second rank appeared behind them, and the first rank began moving down the slope, the first Asbalnian arrows flew.

Even constant practice, with the amount of time the Warriors had been allowed, could not make every man a skilled archer. Most, however, were capable of making a fair number of arrows count, at such short range.

But even deadly archery could do no more than to break somewhat the impact of the charge, and the Warriors had to stand to meet them, sword in hand. It soon appeared that a determined infantryman could hold his own against even a mounted man, for a jab at a horse's face with a sword would often cause him to turn away, making any fighting ability of his rider less effective.

After a few minutes, the Hygerian cavalry withdrew.

THE WARRIORS HAD a little time to make ready before the Hygerian infantry attacked, and they made use of it. A few went out to collect what arrows they could salvage from the field, while Rorick discussed tactics with Beran and Dolan, The first Hygerian infantry force amounted to about four hundred, and was intended to sweep the small Asbalnian force away to let the main body through. Swift arrows decreased their numbers somewhat, but many of them reached the Asbalnian ranks.

It had taken some time, but those who ruled the Hygerians had finally realized that the only thing to deal on equal terms with the well-trained disciplined Asbalnian infantry would be equally well-trained and disciplined Hygerian infantry. They had begun, from that time, to treat their infantry as actual troops, rather than as inferior persons who did not or could not ride. As a result, their infantry was now becoming a force to be reckoned with.

The Asbalnians shot their last arrows when the Hygerians were forty yards away, to allow themselves time to prepare shield and sword. At the same time, the Hygerians paused to launch their javelins; a thrown missile can be easily dodged, and most were, but with so many in the air, some found their targets. A moment later, with a horrific clashing of metal, the battle joined. Rorick's front rank met them and slowly withdrew before them. The centre rank was moving slowly forward as well, and the attackers, their impetus somewhat broken by the ragged front rank, halted altogether when the fresh centre rank stepped through the front rank.

Though the Hygerians were fierce and valiant, this was too much for them; they fell back, somewhat fewer than they had come.

“They will come again,” said Dolon, “and we have no arrows left to slow them.”

“We must collect their throwing-spears,” answered Rorick.

“Dolon, your men will take the front rank. Throw your spears when they come to about twenty yards, then you and your men shall crouch down while we behind you each throw another spear. You will then rise and charge into them, while the rest of us stay behind to fight whenever we might be needed.”

Chapter Twenty-Eight

When Rorick led his Warriors to the Notch, it was in full expectation that few of them would return. It was a gamble, a gamble which could let the King win the war, for it would take only a few men from the Asbalnian host, and yet would delay Sharakh in the Notch long enough that his arrival could make no difference in the battle.
-The Hygerian War
Randell of Avantir

The Warriors gathered spears quickly, looking a little nervously toward the hill over which the attack would come. They were not left alone for long. Fortunately, the Warriors were allowed time to take up their positions again. Rorick set twenty men aside, formed into a wedge, and told them, "When I need you, I will need you immediately, and without delay. See that you watch me all times."

The Hygerians came shouting over the brow of the hill, a dark wave intent on swamping the Asbalnians. Suddenly, they checked and cast their javelins. The Warriors answered them, and several of the Dark ones went down.

Then came Rorick's shout, and the front rank crouched as javelins whipped overhead. This move caught the Hygerians by surprise, and several of them fell. Then Dolon's men were up and into them. In the first clashing minutes, Rorick saw an opportunity. He called to the men in the wedge, "Follow me!"

Waiting only so long as it took them to form nearly at his back, he rushed forward. They pushed through the Asbalnian ranks, directly into the Hygerians beyond. Rorick pushed forward, not attempting to engage anyone yet, merely forcing his way in. Now, amid the Hygerian force, there was a wedge of Asbalnians, pushing them all out of formation, discouraging them after the last volley of javelins and Dolon's charge had halted them.

It was not over in an instant by any means, for these were the new Hygerian infantry, determined to prove their abilities. But though they fought fiercely, the wedge of men within their formation fought as fiercely as the Mountain Dwarfs. At last, leaving their dead piled behind them, they withdrew.

But they were not broken.

RORICK LOOKED DOWN to the valley where the Hygerians were attacking again, infantry in the centre, cavalry advancing on the wings. They intended to destroy the Asbalnian flanks by cavalry attacks, and exploit it with their infantry.

Then the warriors were under attack again. All Rorick's men, now half-strength or less, were wounded to some degree or another, while there were in the Hygerian force men who had not yet fought at all. Again the javelins flew. Lywan, the standard-bearer, though he warded off two, still fell with one in his throat.

Yet before the standard had leaned an arm's length, Dolon had caught it and bore it forward suddenly into the face of the Hygerian's charge. As they gathered in a swirling knot around him, he planted the pole firmly in the earth and fought.

Rorick, caught by surprise, suddenly realized what it was that Dolon was attempting. He shouted, "Form around your standard!"

It was enough to bring the warriors forward in another determined rush, and they flung themselves into the fray behind Rorick, who wielded the Sword with a skill and ferocity, which made him the first to reach Dolon. Beran was only just behind him, and the rest of the Warriors were nearly with him.

Even as they fought, Beran stumbled backward, then fell, with his sword still buried in the man who had wounded him. Already the Hygerians were leaving the fight, and shortly the Asbalnians held the field alone.

Rorick counted his men; fifty-three remained on their feet.

Chapter Twenty-Nine

Taken as a group, the losses suffered by the Warriors in the notch were proportionally the highest on the Asbalnian side.

On the Hygerian side, whole companies of infantry and whole squadrons of cavalry, threw themselves into battle when the battle was lost.

Courage they had in plenty, and courage in this battle tempered with more reason than hitherto, but it was not enough. Had they been able to see the wisdom of seeking another day, the war would have gone on longer, perhaps to a different end.

-The Hygerian War
Randell of Avantir

Rorick spared another look into the valley; the Asbalnians outmanoeuvred the Hygerian cavalry, driven from the field or crushed into the flank of the infantry to turn them into a confused and straggling mass. The last of their infantry was being thrown in, however, so the issue remained yet in doubt.

Then, far off, coming round the comer of the Forest of Chaldin, there appeared about a squadron of cavalry. Though the distance was great, they appeared to be dressed in Asbalnian fashion.

But he had too much to be concerned with here. His men were gathering Hygerian spears again, and he had given them orders to form a circle when the barbarians came again. They were ready none too soon, for suddenly, Hygerian spears were falling among them.

The Warriors answered them, and Rorick looked to right and left at the men in the circle. “Ah, well, who wants to live forever?”

Hygerians surged against them on all sides, and battle raged and clanged. The circle shrank slightly, and Rorick was standing with Dolon on his left hand. The Hygerians seemed to withdraw momentarily, before flinging themselves forward again with increased ferocity, and in that second Dolon said, “They are all around us now, and are determined that we should die!”

Rorick shrugged and answered, “They have left themselves little room to escape us, then.”

The thought came to his mind of Young Tumell, dead under a Hygerian spear on Avantir’s walls so long ago. The jest leaped from man to man around the ring, and the men smiled as they fought.

There was room, now, for the Dark ones to push past to the plains below. Had that been their wish, but it appeared that they wished to destroy the host of the Guardian’s Warriors. It was, in all likelihood, a tribute to them for having caused the failure of the Hygerian plan. All that remained now was for the Warriors to continue the fight as long as possible, for it was clear that they would not leave the Notch alive.

The battle’s noise was so loud that the sound of hooves only reached them at the very moment that they realized men were coming up the Notch from the Forest side. Through the surrounding foes, Rorick caught a bare glimpse of the Upraised Sword banner flaring back in the wind, and Donal the Bane, face set, lance poised, leading the charge.

The densely-packed mass of Hygerian warriors held solidly for only moments, then broke apart under the pressure. The fierce determination in them melted in the face of this fresh attack, and about four hundred of them fled the field.

Of the Guardian’s Warriors, twenty-one would march down from the Notch. Of the remainder, six were wounded but would probably recover, and twenty-three were wounded near to death, and could be only bandaged and prayed for.

Donal and his men pursued the Hygerians only to the top of the rise, then returned to give a formal salute to

Rorick and his men. Donal dismounted and looked into Rorick's eyes. "Hail, Guardian. It would seem that we came only just in time."

"And what of my orders to stay in Avantir?"

"We were none of us happy at being left behind, and with those who had been wounded and recovered, and with those newly recruited, there were enough to keep Avantir safe The news of Hardinian came to us, we cast lots and the winners agreed to mutiny. We took the best horses we could find, rode through the Guardian's Pass, bypassed Coerl, and rode overland to here.

"When we saw the Sword banner here at the Notch, we rode like the Hunt of Dyn Fawr to reach you."

Dolon, bone-weary and bloody, his mail hammered to rags, leaned heavily on the staff of the banner beside his Lord, and a slight smile touched his lips as he looked at Donal. "Mutineers all," he declared sternly, and added, "Yet never did I see so loyal a band of mutineers."

Rorick laughed as well. "Well, my most loyal mutineers, hear the sentence of your punishment; you shall aid us in finding all those of our comrades that remain yet alive here, and those shall you transport to our camp below, that the wise men and magicians may care for them."

"It shall be done, Milord."

Down in the valley, the remnants of the Hygerian host were fleeing in the direction of the city of Coerl, leaving behind, among the many dead, the dream of the Hygerian Empire.

Rorick cast his eyes over the field where he stood, where those who remained of the Warriors were at work making litters, and gently laying upon them those of their comrades who were wounded and yet lived.

He wandered among them, telling off in his mind silently the roll of the fallen men known well to him, comrades of long marches and hard fights. At last, he took a seat on a boulder. Dolon, coming to consult with his commander, noticed the tears in his eyes, but said nothing of them. Perhaps it was because of the tears in his own eyes.

"Milord Guardian, what are we to do with the Hygerian wounded, whom they have left behind?"

"Care for our own first, then do what you can for the Hygerians. Has there not been enough and to spare of butchery here today?"

THE GUARDIAN AND his Warriors wended their way slowly to the valley, and as they came down, Conel and Phedron rode over to meet them. Phedron had lost one of the wings on his helmet and bore a slight gash on his right thigh. Conel had only a few scratches, but his shield was thoroughly battered.

"Hail, Guardian, and hail also to your Warriors. You have bought this day the freedom of our people."

"Hail to you also, Milord King. You have not stood by while purses were being opened, either. You will not have them pursued?" Conel viewed the surrounding field, where the corpses of the Hygerians were piled high, with no few Asbalnians among them.

"Pursuit? Enough and more than enough have died this day. They are leaving Asbaln, though there may be among them a few fanatics who will fight until death. Those we will deal with when we must, but we will not seek to increase their numbers by pursuing so closely that desperation drives out fear. Bring your men down, and we will make camp."

"So shall it be. Yet we have a thing to be done first; Beran fell upon the Notch, and he shall be given to the Herofire."

Down beside the forest, they gathered wood for the pyre. When it was of sufficient size, they laid Hygerian weapons atop it, and set the body of Beran on that. Rorick himself set the torch to the pyre, and as the flames leaped to seek the darkening sky, he sang. The song was a Hero-song, of the sort that had been sung 'ere the Old Island burned and sank:

"Hear my song of stern strife, song of men of war;

Hear a song of Swift Beran, who will return no more.

Fiercely riding foemen came, Gunn of Asbaln fell;

Dark cloaks walked each city wall, sought each wood and dell.

Conel, in the Hills concealed, called for men to fight;

Avantir fell in bitter battle, a bloody night.

Came the Sword to Conel's side, came to raise the land;

Came the heir of Ralf Starblade, with his little band.

Swift men from the Hills rode, raided to the plain;

In the Hills a hidden army learned to fight again.

When at last they sought a battle, who stood at their head?

Who but he who taught them, he who ever led?

Yea, Beran the Swift, the Loyal, bearing blade to fight,

Woe to us who mourn you, on this cheerless night!

Leaping flames to skyward, honour thus our friend

Who in this dread battle met his foreseen end.

Dreary blows the wind of autumn, mournfully and chill;

Sere and the grass lies, dying on the hill.

Green will grow the grass in spring, flowers find rebirth;

But no more will Beran the Swift walk upon the earth."

As the pyre burned down, and darkness grew, they saw around them the sparkling of other fires. Some were the fires of the camp where the weary host prepared to eat and sleep, but others marked where fallen warriors were being honoured as Beran was.

PRIOR TO RETIRING for the night, Rorick took a turn through the camp, according to his usual habit. On his way, he passed through the tents where the wounded were being kept. As he approached, he met a man leaving; after a moment he recognized Brioghir, son of Cadda, his dark young face set and grim.

"What brings you here, son of Cadda?"

"My father is wounded once more, and it has fallen to me to bear him word that Dannan lies dead on the field. If this be the victory you sought, Milord Guardian, then dearly was it bought."

"So are most victories, Brioghir, and I say it who have left friends and comrades and family on many fields since first I drew sword in battle. Yet we have regained the mastery of our land, and this we must call worth the price that was paid."

Chapter Thirty

Two Kings in the courtyard fight,
Sword and dagger in the morning light.
Nigh is the prize: The throne of the land,
And victory goes to the swiftest hand.
Dark King moves with skillful sword,
Watching and matched by the Golden Lord;
Iron ringing of the parried blow;
Is musical measure as round they go.
-from 'The Battle of the Kings' Rorick of Avantir

Early the next morning, one of Phedron's young swordsmen, a lithe and slender man, wakened Rorick. Though it had been freshly painted since the previous day, his shield had already seen much wear.

"The King wishes to speak with his leaders, Milord Guardian."

If Rorick had doubted his Northland origin, his speech confirmed it.

"I shall be there presently."

Rorick was the first to reach Conel, who was seated outside his tent, in deep thought. "What is it, friend? Our scouts report fresh armies of Hygerians?"

"No, rather the road west from Coerl is filled with Hygerians, men, women, and children, fleeing to someplace beyond our wrath."

"So, why do we meet so early? The war—host cannot move today."

"It is this that I wish to discuss. But let us wait for the rest."

Already Phedron was striding up, looming as large off a horse as he did on, with the lesser captains straggling behind him. Rorick noted that a full third of these had been seconds-in-command yesterday, near as many were newly promoted from the ranks since yesterday.

Conel looked around at them. “The scouts have said that the Hygerians are fleeing from the city of Coerl. I am minded to seat myself on the throne of my fathers as soon as may be; clearly, if we wait until tomorrow we will see no opposition, yet I would rather it were settled today. Tell me now, not what I wish to hear, but what is the truth? If march to Coerl today, how many could I bring with me?”

There were some moments of discussion amongst the captains, then Phedron finally reported. “There is no question of moving so many wounded in case of raid or attack on them, so they must be guarded; altogether, we could menace a force of about twenty—five hundred.”

“So. And again, with no smiling faces on frowning facts, can we march safely to Coerl with this many?”

This question was directed mostly at Rorick and Phedron, who requested first to be allowed to speak with the scouts who had come in since morning. It became clear questioning these that the Hygerian war—host had ceased to exist as a host, every man being concerned with the safe removal of his household and goods from within reach of the King’s host.

“Milord Prince, we feel they would fight us only if we forced it upon them, and even then, they are very disorganized to fight even the force we will bring.”

Conel bowed his head in thought. After a moment, he raised his head and spoke to them. “It may be that I am over—proud, or that I on jealous of my rights, but I have waited over—long since the death of my father to take place on the throne. Some have called me King, these many years, but we know all that am not truly King until I sit on the seat of Gunn, of Coerl, of Conel the Wild gather the men, bring no man who is not willing to march, we so as soon as you can be prepared. Rorick, will your Warriors serve as bodyguard for the both of us?”

"With the greatest of pleasure, Milord King."

"Or at least, with the minimum of displeasure, if I know soldiers," answered the King, his smile returning now that matters were settled.

DESPITE CONEL'S DESIRE for speed, night found them still some five miles from Coerl. A trifle impatiently, he agreed to camp for the night, but on the next morning was waiting for the rest of them with only slightly disguised irritation.

As they approached the city, they discovered that the great movement westward had not ceased. The road was covered with men, women, and children, carts piled high with goods and furniture. A squadron of cavalry, magnificently decked out in black leather adorned with gold, formed themselves in the path of the Asbalnian force, and waited.

Rorick and Conel attempted to parley, promising no harm to anyone if they would not force a fight. The commander made his slight frame seem imposing as he spoke to the two who faced him, casting a dark—eyed stare across his hawk—nose as he answered, "Where should we go, and in what place might we stay? For we are the men of the King of Hygeria, and Hygeria has no king this day. Be sure that we shall not hear men say, 'They live, but their King is dead.'"

It was almost with regret that Conel led the skirmish which destroyed that force, nor was it an easy battle, for they fought bitterly and to the death.

On their entrance to the city, they found some degree of chaos ruling, for while the Hygerians strove to escape, certain Asbalnians, emboldened by the approach of their victorious Ring and his war—host, displayed a ferocity they had not shown before. They began to fall upon the fleeing families to plunder their belongings.

The first sight to greet Conel's eyes inside the gates was a pair of overturned carts, with a family of five lying scattered around them. "This must be stopped," the Prince declared. "Phedron, arrange patrols through the streets. The perpetrators of such deeds are to be warned once. If they do not heed, then use whatever force is necessary to stop them."

With his small bodyguard, Conel continued through to the Palace. It stood out, with a large courtyard before it, and a flight of broad stone steps led up to the great doors. These doors, worked in wood, were produced by the Dwarf Siolbhan, at the request of Coerl. Dobghal, the brother of Siolbhan, bound the doors in bands of iron, with runes of protection upon them. On the inner faces of the buds, so that one must rend the doors in sunder to read them, he wrote in the Dwarfish runes. On the outer faces, the same things were written in the Elder Runes of Cymruthair, for the Dwarfs are loth to let their tongue be written for any to see, save their folk alone.

Yet such was the skill of their craftsmanship that no man looked upon those doors without being moved by the wonder of them, and the fairness and beauty which could be crafted into such common materials.

At the top of the stair stood a single man, but all eyes turned rather to the man at their foot. He was tail, slightly broader than Rorick, with glittering dark eyes and a beak of a nose. His right hand absently fingered his thick black beard. His attire was typically Hygerian; close—fitting black trousers, black cloak fastened at the right shoulder, a leaf—shaped golden brooch lying over a light red tunic. He wore a close—fitting iron cap for a helmet, and a long sword and dagger hung at his waist. He bore no shield. There was not a man among the Asbalnians but knew or guessed him to be Razak, late King of the Hygerians.

As the Asbalnian party drew to a halt before him, he looked up at Conel with a critical eye. "So this is the boy—king of Asbaln? Well, boy—king, you have defeated the hosts of Hygeria, but there is yet a thing to be done. Come now, and fight for your kingdom."

Conel did not move immediately. "Aye, you do well to fear me," declared the Hygerian, "but I care not if you wish to use your shield as well. I care not, so long as you will come to measure swords with me."

The Prince turned to his men. "Let it be as he wishes; the two Kings shall here do battle, and let no men interfere, save at his peril."

He dropped from his horse lightly, leaving his shield, and drew his sword and dagger. Razak came at him in a sudden leap, but Conel was not a slow man. Back and forth they moved, the sun gleaming silver on sword and helm, sparking off darting dagger—tips.

It was an even fight, for Conel was skilled in the use of the sword, with or without shield, and he knew the use of the dagger as well. On the other hand, the use of sword and dagger together was a time—honoured tradition in Hygeria; only Conel's slightly greater speed saved him from Razak's greater skill.

For a time, the fight went so, each attacking and warding in turn, then both circling to look for an opening. Finally, having fallen back about six feet from each other, they paused momentarily. In that moment, Razak's dagger hand moved, and the dagger was a flash of silver in the air as it flew. Conel, dodging, was still wounded in the left arm, but at the same time he was bringing his sword up to ward off the following attack of the Hygerian.

A moment later, clutching at a gashed and bleeding left arm, he stood over the dead body of the greatest King of Hygeria.

Somewhat wearily, he saluted his fallen enemy, then turned to give orders. "Let him be given funeral honours after the manner of the King's of Asbaln. He was a great man and a great leader, though I can only find myself grateful that he is dead. Now, do you who followed me in battle follow me to my throne?"

In this moment there was a pounding of hooves, and the chief magician came dashing up on a white horse to fling himself from the saddle and shout, "Milord King, do not go in there yet!"

"And why not?"

Flinging out a hand, the Old One pointed to the Palace stair. At its head, where the other Hygerian stood, there was a pillar of black smoke. The smoke disappeared suddenly, revealing the Hygerian once more as he made a downward motion with his hands. There was a momentary shimmering in the air, and he had disappeared.

"What does this mean, Old One?"

"A spell has been cast, Milord King. What evil this one has wrought, I cannot yet say, though I have my suspicions."

He looked around, then picked up a javelin dropped in some Hygerian soldier's hasty retreat. He chanted over it, in the tongue of the Arkh-bazd Whazar:

"Akh—dazar lepta fashish noh

Dagah mazadikh khosh ferdo

Kuzadh ligash danodh do

Hashgikh falghikh.

O Asbrodaho!"

Having done this, he cast it in the direction of the place stair; yet before it had come much more than half—way, there was a flash of brilliant light, and the spear disappeared. As the Asbalnians alternately rubbed their eyes and stared, Rorick and Conel approached the old magician.

"What has been done here, Old One?"

"A barrier, Lords. In the time that the two spells interacted, I could see much of what made it. It is a harsh spell, for twenty—seven men were killed to forge it. Thrice, thrice, three lives spent to gather the power for its making. It could be nullified by an equal number of lives, with a proper counter-spell, though such is not our way.

"The fastest way to remove it would be for someone to go in and slay he who stands on the inside. Other than that, it will require much work on the part of myself and my colleagues to clear this away, if we are indeed able."

"If you are able?"

"It is a spell with which I am not familiar, but it may be that this spell will set itself finer with every day in which it is not broken. But it is strange, strange indeed, that this magician should lock himself within the barrier. I suspect it to be a trap, a means to draw someone within the barrier, and either slay or snare them there."

"But such a careless trap. It might take anyone."

"Not really, Milord King. Would you truly send someone else behind the barrier? Who else can say the same, save perhaps one of the Old One's colleagues?"

"The Sword is a defence against many things, and I think it might be surer defence in this case than anything any of my colleagues might attempt. The danger is that the breaking of the barrier may rend space and time, and for one to find his way back here, some Power will be needed, a Power which will draw itself back. I think the Sword may well be that Power."

With the Old One supporting Rorick, Conel yielded, though it went against his desire.

Chapter Thirty-One

Their raiders descended from the mountain refuge, and from the upland hiding-places came their bands. Therefore we resolved to end for all time the little people.

Yet we came to the others, the green ones without cities, taller and stronger than our greatest man. Few are their numbers, but they fight as though they were many. Several were slain as being of no account, some were killed as beasts of no worth, and now they make common cause against us with the little ones in the mountains.

With magic, we fight and do battle by sorcery, but this war will not be won easily.

-from The Writings of Thure Hezim-dher collected by Ammerlyn

They waited now for the rest of the Asbalnian magicians to arrive. As they waited, they discussed matters.

"Is this barrier similar to that within the Icarian pass, Old One?"

"Similar, but different, Milord Guardian. That in the Pass was an unnaturally strong of one such as we commonly use in Asbaln. This one is distinctively Hygerian and differs from all we know.

"It is said by Ammerlyn, the Wandering Wizard, that such barriers as we use disturb the borders of space and time, so that whoever would win through to the central crystal must fight against things of a strange and dreadful nature. It is also said that a form of it was used among the Arkh-bazd Whazar as a test for chieftainship; a man who could win through to the centre was worthy of being followed."

"What can you tell me of the Arkh-bazd Whazar? They are but names to me, but names I have heard often."

"In the Icarian Hills, and in some tales of the Lowlands, you will have heard of the Bowmen in the Iron Coats. They were the Arkh-bazd Whazar. They came to these lands from afar, and were mostly destroyed in their war with the Dwarfs of the Mountains, who allied at last with the Other People. The Other People you will know as trolls. "

"Trolls? in war? They are but animals!"

"That is a part of the story. You know that our ancestors fled to the land east of the Mountains when the Old Island died in the Night of Fire. They settled in the midst of the people who already lived there, the Derrakos who were skilled hunters, and did not stay long in one place. These hunters formed an implacable hatred for the farmers, for they feared for the survival of the game, which was their livelihood. And certain of the farmers gave them further cause, placing homesteads on certain sites where the hunters were known to camp, taking them by right of force.

"So it was, raid and skirmish and uneasy truce, until the coming of the Bowmen in the Iron Coats. They made war on the Dwarfs Who possessed all of this plain on which we stand. By arms they were driven to take refuge in the mountains, but they raided fiercely into the lowlands, causing the Bowmen to resolve to exterminate them.

"They ran afoul of the Other People, who dwelt on the lower slopes, without towns or cities, and in their arrogance, they treated them as they had the Dwarfs. In this manner, they drove the two races into common cause, and thus allied, they proved bitter foes to the Bowmen.

"They therefore sent a small force around the Mountains by ship, to attempt an attack from the rear. Yet their arrogance betrayed them once again, and they pillaged and slew both farmers and hunters for their supplies. It was then that Icar, of whom you will have heard much, gathered a force of both hunters and farmers and defeated that host of the Bowmen.

"Then, foreseeing what the end would be to the conflict over the Mountains, he led all who would follow him into the Hills. The Derrakos withdrew to the Swamp, and the only ones who remained upon the plain were certain of the more stubborn farmers who inherited the land after all was done.

"For in the last stages of that war, both sides let loose wizardries and sorcerous weapons better not used, until at the last, the Mountain Allies blasted all this plain with a magic fire which is called the Little Sun. Town, city, and village were destroyed, the plain was blackened, and the Arkh-bazd Whazar no more.

"Then came the Dwarfs from the Mountains to look upon their homeland. Seeing the blackened desolation and blasted ruins, they turned their faces in grief to the Mountains, whence they have not come again. The Other People, greatest and least, went insane, and have been as beasts ever since. Some say it was a punishment of the High Powers for using such dread weapons, others say that the great evil they had wrought overbore their peace-loving souls."

By now the rest of the Asbalnian magicians had come, singly and in small groups, and they discussed just how and in what manner they were going to work. At last, they came to a consensus of agreement, and prepared to work.

Chapter Thirty-Two

What passed beyond the barrier at Coerl is not known; Rorick knew his own part, but what happened after, and how it so occurred, is a matter on which the Wise can only speculate.
-Book of the Sword
Kerran Berandis

As the magicians, in their circle, took up a low chant, the Old One called Rorick over for his last instructions. "It will need the work of all of us to make the opening. I will nod to you when it is time to go. You will see the entrance, and you must step swiftly. For your life, do not touch the Sword until you are through."

Rorick nodded and stood waiting. The circled wizards continued their chanting, a low murmur inaudible to most of those standing by. Yet regularly in the chant, their voices would rise, and the words of the refrain would sound clear in the courtyard:

"Cylch iranuoth, tenhielen,

Illotu lynta temhielen,

Tel guallanue helffta!"

And ever, as their voices rose, they seemed to take on a new aspect; those who beheld them saw glimpses as of Elder magicians, magicians such as those who lived and wrought in the old days, 'ere the world was changed.

Phedron, standing at Conel's elbow, spoke softly. "So it was the Elder Folk sang, in those far days when first they battled against the darkness." He looked at Conel, who was regarding him a trifle strangely. "Do not your own singers sing of this, or is this lore found only in the North?"

Before Conel had the opportunity to answer, there was a glowing shimmer in the air before the magicians. As all watched, this grew in size and brightness until it was the size of a man and so brilliant that one could scarce look on it.

It was then that the Old One nodded. Rorick stepped quickly forward; he was not sure how to describe the sensation after, though he felt something which would have hindered him, had he hesitated, and he felt a sudden warmth at his side where the sword hung in its sheath. He was standing at the foot of the stair, looking up at the Hygerian standing there.

The warlock's smile was cruel and triumphant. "Rorick of Avantir! Welcome! Welcome! I had hoped to take your King, but you will do, both as an object for revenge and an injury to him. I have heard too much of you, and I like it not, yet even should your fortune smile upon you to the extent of your slaying me, still I doubt your ability to return to your own place. So die, fool!"

Rorick had drawn the Sword upon first sighting the magician, so he was prepared when the Dark one raised a shining ebony rod in his right hand, and struck with it as one might swing a whip. Like a whip indeed came a bolt of lightning, but Rorick had flung up Sword into a parrying position, and the lightning disappeared against that gleaming blade.

Rorick began to bound up the steps, with two thoughts in mind; he must guard himself from the wizardries by the Sword, and he must come close enough to strike the Dark one down. Twice more the dread bolts struck at him, and twice more the Sword turned them to naught.

And after the third one, the Sword itself struck back; a bolt of power smote the Hygerian, slaying him where he stood.

Rorick stared down at him, then glanced at the Sword in his hand. "Now, Old One, let us see if you were correct about the power of the Sword drawing me home again." Turning, he stepped down the stair once more.

At his first step, the world shivered and shook, and ceased to be the world he knew.

CAEL OF THE VERSEK looked down the valley where the Baca were gathering for their final charge. Of the three hundred who had come with him originally, only twenty remained, and behind them the People were still passing through the Gate. One thing remained to do.

He turned to the twenty. "Go, now, I send you forth. When next they come, we few could in no way halt them, but if I remain alone, I may delay them."

One of the boldest bowed. "How will you do this?"

"I will give myself to Tralth. Yes, even I who have ceased to give the Bloody One honour these many years. Do you not think that, to gain my soul, he will hide the last of our folk as they pass the gate? Go and think kindly of me hereafter."

And such was the force of his personality that they turned and went away, leaving him. The Baca began their advance, and Cael spoke the dread words of summons, asking for the aid of Tralth in keeping the Big Men from coming upon the People as they fled, offering in exchange himself.

A thick darkness quickly rolled forward from behind him, and he could no longer see the foemen coming.

ICAR, SON OF VARINDEN, captive in the Dark Lord's cavern, considered the sword which he had been caused to forge. In his wrath after the destruction of his father's farm by the Hunters, he had been taken by the Dark Lord's servants. Fine and careful words had been put before him, and he had been led to see himself, bearing the blade which he would make by the Dark Lord's instructions, smiting foes and righting many great wrongs.

He would take the great sword, and with it he would make a kingdom here, a kingdom in which he would rule all things, and see that all was done according to right and justice. The things he had done to forge the blade, even the most dread of them, he had made right for himself by declaring that it would lead to a later and greater good.

But the placing of the dread runes upon the blade had driven all the fair lies into the open, revealing what stood behind them.

The sword itself would ensnare him. Now, it would bind his soul to the purposes of the Dark One, and he would never be free. A King he would very likely be, but a King in thrall to a force of dread intent.

The creatures of the Dark Lord, jubilant for the completion of the sword, capered and sang.

Icar stood, determined to free himself at any cost. The eye of the Dark One turned to him, and he fell to his knees as though pushed down by a hand of great might. With his hands on the hilt of the sword, its point against the cavern floor, he prevented himself from falling to his face.

Almost unthinking, he cried out: *"Andrythn Athantirnhucathu, illnha tal!"*

Above the door of the cavern, closed by a vast gate of timber, a pinhole of light struck down, gleaning upon the runes on the blade.

The runes writhed and shifted, and were no longer terrible, but rather shone with a light and a glory which brought Icar to his feet, crying in his own tongue, *"Andrythn, Bringer of the Stone of Hope, my thanks!"*

He knew that the terrible deeds done for the forging of the Sword would have to be repaid, but he knew, too, that the payment would not give joy to the Dark Lord. The sword gleamed as he strode to battle.

CONEL THE WILD, in the flickering firelight, addressed the men of the assembled clans of Avantir, on the eve of battle against the Hygerians.

"Two days ago, we fought the Dark ones, and you allowed me to lead you very near to victory. Yet we must fight again tomorrow, because each man, each leader of a clan, is jealous of his own rights. Each one who owns a banner and leads men insists *he* is the wisest of all, and must judge when his men nay follow the orders of anyone else.

"Each of us bears a banner. Each of our clans traces its lineage back to the great Lords of the Old Island, and each insists that his family is greater, is more to be respected for its past deeds, than any other.

"If that be the argument, then let it be said and remembered now that my lineage traces back to Morinden the Fair, last great King on the Old Island.

"Yet there is another and more pressing need, and it camps out there in the night. It wears a black cloak, and it will eat us like a fair red apple, one bite at a time, if we stand not together. Tell me, when you have chosen a war-leader before, have you ever had so much success with so little loss? Lend to me your support, and under this banner," he swung his Red Dragon up to the skies, "We will face and conquer any host of barbarians. Who will follow me?"

The chieftains rose to their feet, shouting.

CONEL OF THE GORTHS, Asbalnian outcast barbarian king, drew the spellsword Worldsdeath from its hiding place. The morning for which Ammerlyn had bid him prepare was upon him, and now the hosts of the Warlock Lord would set forth against them. When the Gorths were conquered, then the hosts of Hotlanders, Nangs, goblins, and other fearful things would be free to descend upon the Second Alliance in the South. Ammerlyn was depending upon the valour of the Gorthic people.

Yet Ammerlyn had said that Worldsdeath was barely equal to the weapons with which the Warlock Lord's host would come down. Conel, who had used Worldsdeath one time, knew its dread power, and had sworn that it should not be revealed again.

He could not, then, ask his people to go out against such forces; he would go by himself, bearing the dread sword, and seek to find and fight the foremost of the warlocks of Vandethair, so that perhaps they would draw back from the Gorthic lands.

He stood and set out walking.

RORICK OF THE IRON HAND stood on Mhoranna Field, surveying the Hosts of Darkness leagued against him. Behind and around him were the armies of the Second Alliance.

The enemy advanced. Rorick drew the Sword and waited.

RORICK OF AVANTIR stood on the Palace steps in the City of Coerl, looking at the King for whom he had fought many battles on so many fields, not always against human foes. For a heartbeat's space, he half-doubted that he was yet home. Then Conel stepped forward, an anxious look on his face.

"Rorick, is it well with you?"

The ground seemed solid under his feet again, and he knew he was back. "Well enough, Conel. The Palace is yours, but do not ask me yet what passed there, for I could not say for sure, and what I could say needs more than a few moments telling. It was as though I were, for a space, both many and one, in several ages. Old One, you have some wisdom and knowledge in these matters; what have you to say?"

"It was a plan of revenge, and it was expected that, even if the barrier could be destroyed, he who did it would not be able to return.

"It was the Sword which saved you, I believe, for it would not let itself be left beyond its own time and place, so it must return. Some powers are not to be denied."

"But what is important is that you are back," said Conel, stepping forward to take Rorick's arm. "You gave me the hospitality of your father's house, and today I repay that with mine. Let us go in."

Chapter Thirty-Three

No mountain high nor storm from the sky
Shall keep me from my lady;
Now the Sword is at rest in the Land of the West,
And I will wed my lady
Close by my side, my battle-friends ride
To bring me to my lady.
To the Hills I go, to a land that I know,
Where shall wed lady.
-From "The Ride to Carill Don"
Dolon, Captain of the Warriors

There were impromptu festivities beginning that very evening, but though Conel first thought that it would be best if he were crowned immediately, he soon came to see that it was necessary to wait, to make proper arrangements, lest it be said that he rushed to the crown with undue haste, lest anyone should deny his right.

Of the old noble families of Asbaln, Rorick only remained. There were a few very distant cousins to the original nobles, but for the most part, the Hygerians had wrought effectively in their attempts to eradicate the leaders of the land.

There was, however, no lack of deserting men among the commanders of the war-host, and much discussion about how the borders of the land might be redrawn.

But all such speculations must wait, for Conel would not even speak of such matters until after the coronation, lest he be accused of buying supporters.

Three weeks later, the coronation was held. One week had been allotted for spreading the word to all parts of the land, two weeks for all who wished to come.

All went well. There was sufficient pomp and ceremony to assure everyone that this was a proper coronation, and there was still enough good-will toward Conel that no one grumbled over any of it. When it was done, and Conel sat on his throne, he called Phedron forward.

"Phedron, you have swung your axe well and nobly in my service, and it is in my mind to reward you fittingly. All the lands of the Seven Hills are yours, to have and hold, subject to your duties to the Crown. Will you accept?"

"Milord King, if it is your will, I will accept. I am likely, though, to prove an unhandy baron for those folks."

"I would sooner have an unhandy baron such as yourself than one who would be unable to hold the land. The Harvatai are nosing around the borders, wondering whether this late war has made us easy pickings yet. Come, take the oath from me."

Many others were honoured in similar ways, and when this was done, the true festivities began.

ALTOGETHER, IT WAS not until about the middle of the fifth week after the entry into Coerl that Rorick was able to speak a private word of farewell to Conel and lead his Warriors out. Some days later, they were winding along the familiar hill-path leading into Carill Don. It was a clear bright fall day, and several of the village women were on its outskirts gathering the roots which, with the meagre crops, would eke out the hunters' meat during the coming winter. They looked up as the Warriors approached, and one exclaimed, "Rorick!"

The little column halted, and Rorick leaped down from his horse; with the Guardian's Warriors and the Icarian women watching, the Guardian of the Sword went to meet his lady.

Epilogue

Rorick, son of Ardan, Guardian of the Sword, went forth against the Derrakos on a day in his sixty-fourth year, and fell in the fighting. Helana of the Hills lived to see her children's children. Randell, the eldest son, took up the Sword after his father; their daughter Lillenni wed one of the sons of Phedron Doubleaxe; Ardan the younger son went wandering, and is said to have passed through the Forbidden Lands, and become a great man in far-off Tharid.

The shield which Rorick had brought from behind the barrier of the pass was never seen again. Those who interest themselves in such things have found several explanations.

From that day on, the Sword never lacked one to wield it, and it came at last to Darkon of Avantir, and to his son, who was Rorick of the Iron Hand.

-Book of the Sword
Kerran Berandis

APPENDIX I

CONCERNING ANDRYTHN DENCLYAN

In the High Days of Old, the Elder Folk lived in the land, which was called Elffanthun, the Elder Home, and were content. Yet the Evil came among them, and they began their long struggle against the Darkness, and great and fierce was that war. Then a time came when younger ones among them wearied of the battle, and questioned why they should continue to strive. For years there was contention among them, and at last a decision was taken.

The Evil Bargain was made, and the Elder Folk, in return for their peace, agreed to give no aid nor succour to Mortal Men, but lately come into the world on the far-off lands.

Yet only barely was the pact made, only barely had the Lords of Darkness left to their new prey, when the Guardians of the World came in wrath. During the long war, they had given aid and counsel often to the Elder Ones, and even the strongest minds quailed at their coming forth. It was hardly necessary to say to the Elder Folk that the bargain they had reached was less than honourable, yet even most who disliked the agreement had concurred in it for the sake of their kindreds.

The Guardians of the World banished the Elder Folk from their beloved Elffanthun until they might redeem themselves by giving aid to Men against the Darkness. Yet for all this, they must be caught in a great and woeful trap, for though the evil pact was a thing of shame, yet had they sworn oaths to said pact, oaths which they must now break, though it would curse much of their enterprise.

And so it proved, for the Dark Ones found Men more ready for their traps, for skilful lies and shining promises, while Men found the Elder Ones strange, a different and distant folk, and few suffered to be allied with them willingly, at the first.

So it was that the Elder Folk fell into despair. When the dangers of the Darkness began to make themselves known, and a few Men were willing to stand with the exiles, the power of the Darkness seemed already invincible.

Andrythn Denclyan, also known as Andrythn Lundell, Andrythn the Ship-maker, purposed to brave the Ban of the Guardians, and seek their aid, for war was clearly preparing, and the Allies were not yet ready.

The trials and difficulties of his journey are set down elsewhere, but to put it shortly, he succeeded. The One called Lhim Lheduan, The Bright Wanderer, returned with him to the shores of Mortal Men, and with them they brought the Athantir, the Hopestone.

Athantir was a message, a symbol that all hope was not gone, and that victory was possible. it was an encouragement not to cease striving, and a promise of light in darkness.

But Andrythn had broken the Ban, and it was forbidden to him to dwell any more with his kindred, and he must roam the seas with the Bright Wanderer for company.

At Mhoranna Field, a battle was fought which destroyed an army of the Warlock Lord, yet the entire power of the Dark Lords was not rooted out and erased; for it had been a great and terrible battle, and there were Kings and Chiefs among men had led the most of their fighting men to battle, and now stood with barely enough for a bodyguard, and there were hosts of men who had come for the sake of loyalty to their leaders, and now saw King or Chieftain dead on the grass.

And very soon, contentions arose between the various groups, and it came nigh to being a matter of blows between late friends, so the host broke up, and went its ways, content with what many knew to be only a partial victory.

When Icar, in his imprisonment, called upon Andrythn for aid, he was calling on one who had done more than most for the uniting of the various branches of the Allies. It is not surprising that his appeal should be answered.

APPENDIX II

PHILOLOGICAL NOTES

This is a section which will be of great interest to some, and of no interest at all to others. It seemed to me, however, that something should be done to point up some of the differences of the various peoples involved. A study of the languages would, as well, add a little background to the total story.

The Elder Folk

The Elder Folk, commonly known as Çymrutha (*Çym*, 'silver' *rutha*, 'tongue.') will take the first place here, though they are mentioned only peripherally in the book, because they have had such a pervasive influence on the other languages, particularly Asbalnian.

The Çymrutha language has some resemblances to Greek or Latin, in that it has a system of cases, and a very much inflected verb. The noun—cases are Nominative, (subject) Genitive, (usually possessive) Accusative (direct object) Dative, (usually indirect object.) I will deal first with the larger phrases of the language, which give some idea of the grammar, then go on to speak of one or two names.

On page 205 we have:

Cylch iranuoth, tenhielen,
Illotu lynta, temhielen,
Tel guallanue helffta.

A word-for-word translation might be:

Ring of danger, break
Work of doom, fail
By the High ones of Old.

Cylch means 'ring,' and occurs also in some places similarly to Latin *'circum—,'* for instance, *cylchath*, 'go around (the edge).'

Iranuoth, from *iranu*, 'danger,' actually means 'dangerous,' so we might also translate 'dangerous ring.' In Çymrutha, though, the adjective usually follows the noun, and I decided to keep the word—order.

Tenhielen is basically a subjunctive, and in this case translates as 'may you be broken.' The root is *nhel*, 'break,' here in the passive stem, *nhiel—*,' be broken.' *Te—* is the second person singular prefix, 'you.' If English still used it normally, it would be translated as 'thou' suffix *—en* indicates the subjunctive.

Using the passive here might seem a little unusual, but the fact is that the active generally was transitive. *Tenhelen* would more likely mean 'may you break (something.)'

Illotu is from the root *ill* 'make, create;' the passive stem is *illo—*, and here a participial ending, *-u* is added. The *-t* is simply added for euphony. *Illotu* would translate, more literally, as 'a thing having been made.'

Lynta is from the noun *lyn*, 'doom, death,'and is in the genitive case, making it essentially an adjective.

Temhielen is another passive subjunctive, based on *mhiel-*, the passive stem from the root *mhel—*, 'fail.' Again, the use of passive seems strange, but it would appear that the passive, In this form, gives a sense of immediacy. 'May you be broken, may you have already failed.'

Tel is a particle of instrumental force, meaning approximately, 'by means of.'

Guallanue, from the roots *guall-* 'high,' and *an*, roughly 'being,' though it also is used in the sense 'person;' *—ue* is the suffix of the dative case, which in this instance indicates that the word is to be taken with *tel*.

Helffta, from the root *helff*—, 'old,' bears the genitive suffix already mentioned under *lynta*.

Next, we will look at the phrase on p. 205. *Andrythn Athantirnhucathu, illnha tal!* Andrythn, Bringer of the Hopestone, your aid!

Andrythn is a name composed of *and*- 'wise,' and -*rythn*, 'heart.'

Athantirnhucathu Athan-, 'hope,' *tir*-, 'stone,' *nhucath*-, 'bring' with the —*u* participial ending. 'The one who brings the Hopestone.'

illnha 'help, aid.'

tal, second person singular possessive pronoun, 'your'(thy.) The fuller meaning of this was explained in Appendix I.

We will now look at some Çymrutha names.

Brhandon (p. 71) *Brha* 'great' *andon* 'wisdom' from and, 'wise.' This is a name of an Elder Wizard.

Thumill (p. 15) 'right,' *ill* 'do' 'Doer of Right.'

Name of an Elder Hero. The Asbalnian *Tumell*, (p. 17) is an Asbalnian colloquial pronunciation of this.

Lhorannon (p. 170) *Llor* 'Bold,' *annon*, form of *andon*, 'wisdom.' An Elder Wizard, though not of the era or of the stature of Brhandon.

Coerl (p. 12). This is an Asbalnian colloquial pronunciation of *Dencoirl*, 'The Foreseen One.' The root *den*, 'one,' gives rise to *denc*, 'first, prior;' the root *or* 'see,' produces the passive stem *oir* 'be seen,' and to this is added an old suffix of generally agentive meaning. This —*l* suffix is not often used, and when found, it is usually in names, which are passed on by tradition.

The name is one given to one of the Kings of Asbaln.

Asbalnian

The Asbalnian language bears a resemblance, in grammatical structure, to Latin and Greek. No actual phrases or sentences of the language come into the book, but some names might be of interest.

Asbaln. *As*, 'west,' *baln*, 'land'

Ilcaniar (p. 14) *Il* 'great,' *caniar*, 'river'

Randell. *Ran* is a dialectical pronunciation of the Çymrutha root *ron* 'sword' *dell* is derived from *lell*, 'white, silver,' the *l* becoming *d* under the influence of the preceding *n*.

Avantir. This is a mystery. Some would derive it from Asbalnian *afen* 'defend,' with Çymrutha *tir*, 'stone.' The difficulty here is that, to change *afen* to *avan* does not agree with the alternations in any dialect known.

Others try to make *avan* into the dative singular of *av* 'this.' The meanings advanced in support of this theory have more to do with imagination than with philological realities.

I wish to discuss only three other names here, *Lagan* (p. 132) *Lughan* (p. 132) and *Lywan* (p. 187). The basic root is *laga* 'tear, rend,' and the first form appears to be the most original. The first *a*, being stressed, underwent changes, first to a short *ŏ* (as in bought) then long *ō* (as in 'coat'). At the same time, the *g* was becoming a velar fricative *gh* (similar to the French *r*), which later developed into *w*. This was probably responsible for the *u* changing to the German *ü*, which I represent in the book as *y*.

In some dialects, of course, none of these chances took place, and in some only a few happened. The result was that it was possible to find: in the Asbalnian war—host, men bearing three variants of the same name.

While speaking of dialect differences, I have noted that the Northland dialect was quite distinctive. Among its other striking peculiarities was the habit of changing combinations of *kw*, *gw*, and so on into *p*, *g*, and so on. Examples of this would be *kwishar*, 'horse,' becoming '*pishar*,' *kwa* 'have,' becoming *pa* and *ghuene* 'hope, becoming *vene*.

In some places this tendency was so pronounced that *go—* or *ko—* underwent the change as well, *Conel* or *Coerl* becoming *Ponel* or *Poerl.*

Some Northlanders, attempting extreme correctness, brought smiles to many faces when they called their country *Asgwaln.*

Arkh-bazd Whazar and Hygerian.

I place these two together because of the relationship between them. They derive from the same stock as the Hotland group of dialects and are grammatically similar to the Semitic languages.

Both races, Arkh-bazd Whazar and Hygerian, appear to have migrated early on from the Hotlands towards the Southern Sea. Some history of the Arkh-bazd Whazar, the famed Bowmen in the Iron Coats, has been preserved, but all that is told of the Hygerians' origins is that they emerged, as two eponymous heroes, from a great cataclysm.

Some see, in this, a reflection of the great destruction wrought at the end of the war between the Bowmen and the Mountain Allies. This is possible, but we must then hypothesize the Bowmen as representing a group of divergent dialects and must assume that only those which did not resemble the dialect preserved in their writings survived the war.

To explain, the Hotland word for make is *wasar.* This becomes *washar* in Hygerian but in Arkh-bazd Whazar it is *wazar*. Phonetic laws would permit *s* to become *z* or *s* to become *sh*, but not a progression of *s* to *z* to *sh*.

The Arkh-bazd Whazar quotations are all in the form of spells, and the grammar in them is, to say the least, unusual. The normal form of the language, as found in the surviving historical and other works, confirms that this is not merely the frustrated reaction of philologists to a slight difficulty in grammar.

I shall therefore simply give the roots involved in the spell on page 83.

Shalak, 'call.'

Deflun, from *de—* 'and,' and *falan*, 'come'. This root is also found in *flonha.*

Trilekh, from *taral*, 'show.' This root is also found in *tirilekh.*

Rodosekh from *radas* 'command.'

It will be clear by now that the Arkh-bazd Whazar word is normally based on a root consisting of three consonants, and that some of the alterations in meaning or grammatical form are achieved by changes in the vowels which separate the letters. It is this feature which brings out the comparison with the Semitic languages. There is less of Hygerian in the book, but that which exists shows less problems grammatically than the Arkh—bazd Whazar.

On page 76 we have *washariba ghelhagir*, 'We do it for the families!'

Washar means 'make, do;' — *iba* is the first person plural ending, 'we.'

Ghel — means 'for, on behalf of.' *Hagir* is 'family.'

It ought to be noted here that the Hygerian's own name for themselves is *Hagirak*. In the Asbalnian pronunciation, the first *a* has been diphthongized into *ai*, and the—*ak* ending replaced by the Asbalnian—*kon*, 'folk, people.' A phonetic representation of this would be *Haigirkon*, but due to the need for constant representation of the name through the book, I have taken a sort of Anglicization of the Asbalnian form, as an indication that it *is* an adaptation into a language of a foreign name.

On page 89 we have *Kadwashribazd*, 'by our deeds:' *Kad*—is 'by means of,' *washri* is a participial form of *washar*, 'make, do,' and *bazd* is the first person plural suffix, 'our.'

Icarian

Under this heading, I include the language of the Derrakos of the swamp, as both languages are basically the same, though the Icarian speech has heavy Asbalnian influence.

Icarian is what has been known as an amalgamating language, which means that various elements are added to the root to alter the meaning, and that often a single word may cover a complete sentence. The closest comparisons to the Icarian speech would be some of the North American Indian languages, the position and structure of the final person—markers resembling the Algonquian family (Cree, Ojibwa, Blackfoot) and the formation of the stem calling to mind the Yuman languages (Yuman, Mohave, Diegueño).

As a first example, let us consider the name of the Swamp,

Korochinda. *Kor* means 'home,'*—och—* is a suffix, never occurring alone, indicating something out of sight, *in* means 'danger,' and the final element, *—da*, means 'no, not.' The total, 'Home—hidden— danger—not,' would probably best be translated as 'Safe Haven.'

Kr Yrriech, 'The earth alone endures,' is composed of *Kr*, 'earth,' *yr*, 'endure, last,' *—ri—*, indefinite progressive particle, indicating action having gone on in the past and continuing to an unspecified time in future, *—ech* 'alone, uniquely.'

Having mentioned the personal suffixes, I should note that the third person singular is marked by the lack of such a suffix.

I should also say that, given the normal structure of the form ought to have the adverbial particle *—ech* in second place, *yrechri*, but certain formal and ritual utterances show that there was a time when the position of adverbal particles was less fixed.

Khabarstymbion (p. 59) 'may you come back in health.' *Kha—*, 'may it be that,' *bar*, 'come,' *stym*, 'well, healthy,' *—bi* (actually *—vi*, the becoming *b* under the influence of the preceding *m*) is a conditional particle, giving a sort of subjunctive sense, 'might.'

About the Author

J. P. Wagner was both a sci-fi/fantasy writer and a journalist. While his editorials and informative articles could be found in publications such as the Western Producer and the Saskatoon Star Phoenix, Railroad Rising: The Black Powder Rebellion is his first published novel.

A self-proclaimed curmudgeon, but known to his family as a merry jokester, his words have brightened many lives. Sadly, J. P. Wagner passed away in 2015 before the publication of Railroad Rising: The Black Powder Rebellion.

While this may be the last book he finished before he died, it doesn't mean that this was his only book. In addition to his career in journalism, he wrote many novels throughout his lifetime. All of these works have been passed down to me, his daughter and now I will share them with you.

Read more at www.revjpwagner.com.

Made in the USA
Monee, IL
31 July 2024

7fb67834-8027-4db3-aae2-e32483227560R01